I0760437

Nineteen Seventy-Two

THE SEVEN BOOK TWO

SARAH M. CRADIT

Cover Design by Sarah M. Cradit
Editing by Lawrence Editing

ISBN: 978-1-958744-25-3

Publisher Contact:
sarah@sarahmcradit.com
www.sarahmcradit.com

Preface

If you're here, you've hopefully started with *1970,* which is where this series, and the remarkable lives of the seven Deschanel children, really began. The threads winding these seven books together are best enjoyed when woven in order.

As with *1970,* I feel it's important to add the disclaimer that I was not alive at any point in the '70s. I was raised on the music, values, and results of that period, coming up in the '80s with a vision of the world that matched what my parents had experienced in that pivotal decade. My musical tastes, then and now, are highly influenced by the music my parents raised me on, and even today I enjoy Pink Floyd, CSNY, Carly Simon, and other artists who shaped this decade, more than just about anything else.

Yet, as with all my stories, it's imperative to me that I get it "right." I leveraged the experiences of people who *did* live through the time, including the memories of my father, George Klepach, and my dear friend Deborah Burst, who not only grew up in the '70s, but in New Orleans, where this story takes flight. She's been invaluable in helping me visualize those experiences unique to New Orleans in that period, such as the incredible music scene of The

Warehouse (before there was a district of the same name), and the allure of the Playboy Club, for my own playboy, Charles.

Any errors, however, are entirely my own. As I mentioned in the last book, research can only take you so far, and where I took contextual liberties in the absence of hard facts, I'll beg your forgiveness if I went too far... or not far enough.

Beyond the setting, beyond the time, is the story, and the story is one only these characters can tell. I'm grateful they've given me the voice to find theirs.

Also by Sarah M. Cradit

KINGDOM OF THE WHITE SEA

Kingdom of the White Sea Trilogy

The Kingless Crown

The Broken Realm

The Hidden Kingdom

The Book of All Things

Blackwood Cycle

The Raven and the Rush

The Poison and the Paladin

Southerlands Cycle

The Sylvan and the Sand

The Flame and the Forsaken

Guardians Cycle

The Altruist and the Assassin

The Belle and the Blackbird

Darkwood Cycle

The Melody and the Master

The Hand and the Heart

Sceptre Cycle

The Claw and the Crowned

The Duke and the Disciple

THE SAGA OF CRIMSON & CLOVER

The House of Crimson and Clover Series

The Storm and the Darkness

Shattered

The Illusions of Eventide

Bound

Midnight Dynasty

Asunder

Empire of Shadows

Myths of Midwinter

The Hinterland Veil

The Secrets Amongst the Cypress

Within the Garden of Twilight

House of Dusk, House of Dawn

Midnight Dynasty Series

A Tempest of Discovery

A Storm of Revelations

A Torrent of Deceit

The Seven Series

Nineteen Seventy

Nineteen Seventy-Two

Nineteen Seventy-Three

Nineteen Seventy-Four

Nineteen Seventy-Five

Nineteen Seventy-Six

Nineteen Eighty

Vampires of the Merovingi Series

The Island

and more

The Dusk Trilogy

St. Charles at Dusk: The Story of Oz and Adrienne

Flourish: The Story of Anne Fontaine

Banshee: The Story of Giselle Deschanel

Crimson & Clover Stories

Available as a single collection, The Shorts

Surrender: The Story of Oz and Ana

Shame: The Story of Jonathan St. Andrews

Fire & Ice: The Story of Remy & Fleur

Dark Blessing: The Landry Triplets

Pandora's Box: The Story of Jasper & Pandora

The Menagerie: Oriana's Den of Iniquities

A Band of Heather: The Story of Colleen and Noah

The Ephemeral: The Story of Autumn & Gabriel

Bayou's Edge: The Landry Triplets

For more information, and exciting bonus material, visit www.sarahmcradit.com

The Seven in 1972

Children of
August Deschanel (deceased) &
Colleen "Irish Colleen" Brady

Charles August Deschanel, Aged 22
Augustus Charles Deschanel, Aged 21
Colleen Amelia Deschanel, Aged 20
Madeline Colleen Deschanel, Deceased
Evangeline Julianne Deschanel, Aged 18
Maureen Amelia Deschanel, Aged 16
Elizabeth Jeanne Deschanel, Aged 13

For Evangeline

SPRING 1972

NEW ORLEANS, LOUISIANA

Prologue: Irish Colleen and the Seven

Colleen Deschanel, known as Irish Colleen to her family and friends, peeked her head into the bedrooms of her seven children, one by one, as she did every night of her life.

When she swung the door open into the room of her oldest, Charles, she curbed her surprise at the lack of his presence. When was he ever there anymore? He'd always come and gone like a fickle specter, and she wondered why he didn't, finally, leave the family home for a life more suited to his desire for lack of law and order.

Next, she checked on Augustus, whose absence was more notable. Her sweet boy, the one who should have been heir. She'd lost Charles years ago, and now she had lost his brother, but while the former was a loss driven by character, the latter was a matter of conscience. Augustus would never lay aside his guilt in Madeline's death, and his only balm was usefulness of another kind. She could call over to his office, but it would be wasted breath. He was there, probably curled up on his couch, sleeping just north of anywhere sound. He'd jump straightaway into work, and with luck, she'd see him at dinner if he let himself pause long enough to eat. She'd set a place for him, anyway, as she always did.

At Colleen's room, nothing was out of order, at least that Irish

Colleen could see with her eyes. Colleen was sound asleep, her blankets lying neatly over her as if she'd slid under them with a mind to avoiding disruption. On her bedside was stacked the heavy pile of textbooks, a strange mix of who Colleen was before and after the loss of her sister. She had always found her meaning in a classroom. Irish Colleen prayed she would find meaning, one day, in a matter of the heart.

She still, even two years later, paused outside Madeline's door. The contents hadn't changed since the night Madeline fled with her anger, and, in the early hours of Christmas, died with it. Irish Colleen's hand trembled at her side. What if she opened it? What if Maddy *was* there, flipping through her crate of records? What if...

Evangeline's snores were a symphony—no, that was far too nice, a word of love, not reality, they were godawful—that carried into the hallway of Oak Haven. Irish Colleen went from seeing them as adorable when her spirited genius was a toddler, and, eventually, for the one thing that might prevent her daughter from ever marrying. Now, though, when nothing was okay, they were a great comfort. A constant in a time of fluidity and change she couldn't ever put her hands around.

Irish Colleen's hand paused on her bedroom door, and then she went on, to Maureen, who was dealing with something she believed her mother to be unaware of. But she was aware now, as she suspected the first time, that her precocious Maureen was involved in things she had no business with at sixteen. She wished, as she did many times in a day, that August were here to help guide her in how to handle each of her unique children.

Irish Colleen opened the door and blew a kiss across the room. Maybe Maureen was sleeping. Maybe she was only pretending. But it was their thing, no matter how things stood between them.

As always, Irish Colleen stopped last at Elizabeth. Her baby, Lizzy. The tortured one.

Moonlight spilled through the dormer window and onto the floor before her youngest daughter's room, a familiar sight that both stilled her heart and reminded it that everything could change in an instant.

Irish Colleen slipped inside the bedroom. She grabbed a deep breath before she rounded the corner, where she could see Elizabeth clearly, and in an instant, gauge whether her sweet girl would be enjoying needed sleep or carrying a great burden.

She would never forget the burden Elizabeth laid upon her the spring of 1970. The spring seemed the worst for Elizabeth. The season of light and flowers was, for Lizzy, a time for the weeds to find their way in through the cracks.

Last spring had been mercifully quiet. But this cursed family wouldn't pass another with such a reprieve. Irish Colleen carried this knowledge with her each night into the bedroom of her youngest, who held the keys to everything.

Elizabeth was not sleeping, but that didn't mean anything was wrong. Irish Colleen let her breath escape in a slow rhythm. Sweat clung to her baby's nightgown, so something *had* happened, that was for sure, but it didn't have to be about them this time. It didn't have to be one of the seven in turmoil again. Elizabeth had made a profession of predicting the misfortunes of her classmates and teachers. It could be anything.

Anything at all, really.

"Lizzy." Irish Colleen gripped her nightgown and sat at her daughter's bedside. "What's wrong, dearest?"

Elizabeth sniffled and looked down at her hands.

"You were quiet at dinner."

"Middle school is tough, man."

Irish Colleen started to respond and then realized this was her youngest daughter's odd, but developing humor about the world. She didn't understand it, or her, at all, but she knew it was better to smile. You smiled when you could in this world. In this family.

"Yes, but you're tougher." Irish Colleen reached into the bedside drawer and pulled out a hair tie. The balls at the end knocked together as she pulled Elizabeth's damp hair tight in her fist, working the odd contraption around the knot. "You're a Deschanel."

Elizabeth shrugged. She swiped her hands across her wet gown, and then giving up on that, leaned against the back of her bedframe. "You're just old."

At this, Irish Colleen did laugh. "Old? Missy, you better be careful there. You'll be my age before you know it."

"Will I?"

Irish Colleen pressed her hand to Elizabeth's cheek and turned her head in a snap. "Don't talk like that. Others can joke like that, Lizzy, but not you. When you say it..."

"Yeah, yeah. You don't know if I'm just talking, or if it's the visions."

"You would tell me, wouldn't you?"

Elizabeth shrugged again and shuddered through a deep breath. "Mama, every time I open my mouth, someone gets hurt. What good is saying it when I can't prevent it?"

Irish Colleen dropped to her knees on the shag carpet. She gripped Elizabeth's slick hands in hers. "Elizabeth, no. You have to tell me."

"I told you before. Maddy still died."

Irish Colleen's eyes stung. She hated to cry... control was all she had, and even that was a fleeting, thin construct that came and went. "Is someone... another one of us going to die?"

Elizabeth sighed and slumped forward. "This isn't going to be our year, Mama."

CHAPTER 1

Love is the Answer. What was the Question?

Charles groaned as the first of the long sleep departed. Something blinded him beyond. He could see this even through his closed eyes. He rolled his head back and forth for relief, but found none. Heat accompanied the sensation, which was heavy, suffocating. The thick layer of crust gathered at the corners of his mouth cracked as he yawned and smacked his gums. The memories of last night's debauchery welcomed him in an array of tastes and flavors, like rings on a tree trunk.

The night started at the Playboy Club, but oh, it hadn't really *begun* until they ended up here.

His limbs screamed as he willed them to action. He pitched forward, moving himself out of the intrusive line of sunlight streaming in. Both hands slid down his face, down his stubble, which was new, but he was older now, and shaving daily was a part of life he'd yet to embrace. His hands came back with a layer of grime that had a story to tell. No doubt whatever oozed out his pores should come with a biohazard warning.

The hotel room was empty. It hadn't been the night before, but the remnants of the party didn't leave with the guests. The hundreds of silvery, glittering beer cans, now empty and scattered, came together in a mosaic of depravity. Condoms littered the furniture and flooring. He chuckled, then regretted it when his solar plexus seized in pain. Had he been in a fight, too? Where were Colleen and Evangeline when he needed their healing hands?

Charles couldn't make himself stand, so he forced himself to fall to the carpeted floor. He grunted on impact and scrambled to his hands and knees. That was better. Just ahead, white dust blanketed the floral pattern of the carpet. Angry, at first—who would discard precious cocaine like that!—but then sensing the opportunity, he scrambled forward, toward the prize, like a crab missing half its legs.

"Give me a few minutes to get him decent, and we'll be out of here. My office will handle the damages."

"Very well."

Was that Colin? Charles buried his nose in the dirty fibers and inhaled. He fell back, coughing and fighting back one hell of a sneeze. He'd taken in some of the good stuff, but also some other things, probably dust, and dirt, and, if Evangeline were here, she'd tell him dust was a collection of broken, discarded bug wings and other—

A golden halo of light appeared before him. He blinked and strained his sight into focus. The halo subsided, but what remained was no less awesome. Cat.

"Huck," she said softly. A hand brushed his greasy hair back from his face. "Rough night, huh?"

Rough? Charles wouldn't have explained it that way at all. His dick might be broken, but he wouldn't be stopping in to visit the complaints department. How did other orgy enthusiasts handle the task? Is that what they were called, orgy enthusiasts? Orgiasts? Orgy connoisseurs? His first foray into this sexual art might have been overkill. Seven women, and he, the only man. His dick throbbed. Yeah, it was broken, but he expected an ad in the Times-Picayune praising his performance.

"Cat, come on, don't baby him. He's not a child."

Catherine dropped into a crouch before Charles. Her smile was pink bubblegum and honey fresh from the hive. "No, but he's hurting, Colin. Don't forget that."

"Forget it?" Colin stopped short of laughing. "His pain is the only thing keeping him out of jail. Anyone else would be in a world of trouble right now."

"He is in trouble, though." She fell back, settling onto her heels. She pressed her palm to his chest. "Aren't you? You just can't see it."

Charles swallowed so hard whatever was trapped from the night before was forced down his esophagus. She said the words as if she could see straight to his heart, right through whatever skin and sinew and bone separated the organ from the air.

"Charles, come on, get up. Cat, seriously, I know you mean well, but we've got to get him out of here before the hotel owners think too hard about the offer I made them. Augustus isn't going to help smooth this one over, not this time."

"You're a good man, Colin Sullivan, but you've never known pain like your best friend has."

"But his siblings have, and they haven't spent the past two years destroying their reputation and every hotel in town. They haven't avoided drug charges… let's see, twelve times?" Colin ticked off his fingers. "What else am I missing? Felony vandalism, public indecency, statutory rape—"

"*Underage sex,*" Charles corrected, belching further evidence into the musty room. Acrid. He raked his teeth over his tongue to rid it of the vile taste. What else had he done last night? Sucked on copper pipes?

Well, he'd sucked on something. That didn't make him a fairy, either. Whatever got the girls wetter was just part of the game.

"Given the consequences of underage sex where you're concerned, I would think you'd take that a lot more seriously."

The daughter out there somewhere. How old would she be now? Over a year. The letter, telling him where. Neither existed anymore. He'd burned the information in the fireplace of the heir's office at Ophélie. "Protection, my man. It's a wonderful thing."

Colin scanned the room in palpable disgust. "From the looks of it, yes."

"Impressive stamina," Catherine whispered with a playful wink only Charles could see, and he very nearly asked her to marry him on the spot.

"Seriously, Charles, we need to get out of here." Colin sighed as his eyes took another trip around the ruined suite. "Now."

"You think you can get up?" Catherine asked. She rocked back on her feet and held her hands out.

For you, I could fly out of here. Charles took her hands and focused all his energies on not stumbling. A man who could create the apocalypse in this room was one who must walk proudly through the wreckage; the great Napoleon, traversing the Alps. No, Caesar. Napoleon was purportedly a little man, at least that's what Charles remembered from the one or two history classes he bothered to attend. There was nothing small about Charles Deschanel.

He was Caesar, crossing the Rubicon.

"Any day now, Gatsby."

"Come on," Catherine coaxed, leading him to his feet. Her smile encouraged him, even though deep down he knew it was the smile of a mother proud of her son for using the potty for the first time.

I don't think I can, he thought, but then he did, because Catherine believed in him, not only in this moment where he was reduced to contrition, but in every moment. She looped her arm through his, and his hand came to a rest on her arm, where he wanted to run his fingers over the soft, blond down, but didn't, because that might be the end of things with Colin.

"What happened yesterday?" she asked as she navigated him through the carnage of last night's shenanigans. That she asked... that she *knew* this had not been just a party, just a release...

Charles swallowed the lump, this one newer, not from the night before. But it was there last night, because it was always there, his constant companion. His reminder.

Look at our mother! Look at that gray! That's you, Maddy! You! You stupid, ungrateful bitch, you are sending our mother to an early grave!

"I saw on the news..." Charles grimaced as his foot came in

contact with an empty beer keg. "They passed an amendment yesterday."

"Yes, the twenty-sixth. Lowering the voting age to eighteen." When Charles stumbled again, Catherine shot Colin a look. He grumbled and came to help. She rewarded him with a kiss.

"Yeah," Charles said. "That one."

"It's great news," Catherine said.

"Great news," Charles repeated. "Would be a lot fucking greater if Maddy had lived to see the thing she worked so hard for."

"Come on," Colin said, but the sting was missing now. "We'll grab coffee at Café du Monde."

"Maybe we skip the beignets, in case Charles tries to inhale the sugar," Catherine said with a sweet laugh and a squeeze to Charles' arm that sent his heartrate to the moon.

AUGUSTUS TRIPPED OVER THE STACK OF INSULATION half-blocking the narrow hall leading to the bathroom. It hadn't been there earlier, and he'd been carefully navigating in the dark since last night while the electricians worked on wiring. He shouldn't be working through the construction. It was a hazard. But who was going to complain? He was the owner and, on paper at least, the sole employee of Deschanel Media. It wasn't like he was going to sue himself.

"Who ordered a lifetime supply of cotton candy?" Evangeline appeared at his side, smacking her bubble gum.

"It's insulation. Helps with regulating heat and cold."

"Isn't that what our air conditioner and heater do?"

"You're the genius. Go research it."

"Don't tempt me. That's my kryptonite, brother."

Augustus frowned at the obstruction. An office under construction was one always in flux, but he regarded the bright pink stack with undisguised hostility even he didn't quite understand. "You can go home if you want. There's not much for you to do until the printing press comes in."

Evangeline scoffed. "I've saved you thousands on cleaning costs. I'm not afraid of getting my hands dirty. Want me to take a shot at installing the insulation?"

"Thanks, but no. We'll leave that to the professionals."

She flexed, though her thick camo jacket didn't budge at all. "If there's a book on it, I can be an expert in no time."

"I don't doubt it," Augustus replied, still frowning. He didn't know why the insulation agitated him so, when cables hung from open ceilings and half the floor was an obstacle course of materials and hardware. But the glaring bismuth pink challenged him, taunting. Daring.

"When *is* the printing press coming in?"

Augustus stepped over a toolbox and leaned into the wall calendar. "A week from tomorrow."

"That's when you'll start hiring people? Writers?"

"I can't hire until the construction is done. Or at least, until the ceiling panels are closed up and the HVAC is in."

Evangeline looked around. "That's weeks, maybe months away."

"I have phone numbers for the writers I want in the first edition. Don't worry, we'll have Deschanel Magazine out by fall." He checked the clock. It was close to suppertime, and he'd skipped evening meal at his mother's three nights in a row. A fourth wouldn't be forgiven. "Why don't you take the streetcar home and I'll meet you in a couple hours?"

"Nah. I'll wait for you to drive me."

His mouth curled. Not quite a smile. "Lazy."

"No, I just prefer not to see Mama go nuclear when you miss dinner again. You're not the one who has to see her. It's terrible. She sprouts horns just above her judgmental eyebrows, and fire shoots out of her—"

"Yeah, okay, Evie. I get it. I'll be there. I promise."

"Just the same, I'll be your escort."

Augustus sighed. "All right, then. You wanna check and see if the shipment of bathroom supplies arrived downstairs?"

Evangeline grinned. "Roger. I'm tired of wiping my ass with newspapers, too." She skipped away and then turned back to add, "Get it? A magazine, wiping their ass with newspapers?"

Augustus blinked.

"You know, it's a metaphor for—"

"Supplies, Evie."

"Right." She skittered off toward the stairs.

Augustus hadn't asked Evangeline for help with his business venture. He hadn't asked anyone, and the lack of asking wasn't unintentional. Deschanel Media was his baby. Born into his imagination when he wasn't even ten, and now coming to a life. A way for him to be his own man, separate of his family. The business had unlimited potential, but his pet project was a magazine that catered to not only the wealthy of New Orleans, but also the artists who might one day be discovered and change literary history. To give them a platform for their voice and access to the patrons who could help them find their futures.

This last part of his dream was the piece he kept to himself. It went over better with his friends and family to simply say he wanted to publish a magazine for New Orleans. *That* they understood. The rest, they never would.

When Evangeline told Mama she was taking a year off before college, it went over like a skydiving walrus. Irish Colleen had a staunchly single-minded view of college. It didn't matter what her children wanted. College was not negotiable, and it was the only path, as she saw it, to any future whatsoever. It was the magic that created futures, and without it, nothing was possible but darkness and despair. For Evangeline, easily the smartest of the seven, the only one who'd ever been skipped ahead in school, to declare herself weary of it was too much for their mother to handle.

But Evangeline had stated quite clearly that her brother needed help, and she was going to help him.

Augustus could have put a stop to it then, with only a few

words. He almost did. For Evangeline's sake, but also, his own need to be alone. To do this himself. But what began as a mild annoyance had turned into genuine help. She had, as she said, saved him thousands in cleaning costs, but she'd done so much more. She was a workhorse, and she asked nothing in return, not even companionship, which was good, seeing as he had none to offer.

There was this other thing between them. Something neither put voice to but hung unspoken in the office and in the spaces connecting every word they shared. They'd been complicit in sending Madeline off that night. Both kissed her goodbye, understanding she couldn't stay, knowing the risks in letting her go. Evangeline was the only one who could relate to the guilt that pushed him forward, farther away from the man he was two years ago.

That was, he supposed, the real reason he couldn't deny her the break. She needed to be useful, and to do it for and with someone who understood her inherent motivation.

Evangeline came flying down the hall, her boots echoing across the bare concrete. "Danger! Red alert! Jettison fuel!"

"What are you on about? Where are the supplies?"

She doubled over, panting, when she came to a halt. "Carolina. Downstairs. Coming up. Couldn't stop it."

Augustus exhaled. He didn't understand where this interest from Carolina had come from, or why. It seemed to come out of nowhere and overnight turned into a full-blown campaign for his attention. "Okay. Thanks."

Carolina Percy sauntered down the hall in her miniskirt and knee-highs, blond hair flowing down out of a headband, the curling ends tickling her small waist.

She was a vision. On some level, Augustus knew this, but he'd descended the levels to one more suitable to his frame of mind, and on this one, she was only Colleen's silly friend.

It was then he noticed the paper bag in her hand.

"Wow, the office is really coming along!" she exclaimed. "Only thing missing is a woman's touch."

Evangeline cleared her throat.

"Can I help you with something?" Augustus managed the words, which weren't as friendly as they should have been, but they were at least in the neighborhood, and that was progress.

"I was hoping I might help you." Carolina's smile lit up the room. It was out of place, like she was. She reached into the bag. Out came a wooden sign, and as Carolina handed it to Augustus, Evangeline read the words aloud.

"*Love is the answer. What was the question*?" With growing bemusement, Evangeline turned to her brother. "Oh, yeah. That's Augustus all right."

Carolina missed the sarcasm. "Do you like it?"

"It's, uh, really nice, Carolina, thank you."

"I'll hang it on the wall across from his desk," Evangeline teased. "So every time he looks up, he'll be overcome."

Carolina smiled, nodding. "Groovy."

Augustus lifted the sign and forced a smile. "Thanks, Carolina. Really."

"So..." She looped her hands together and rocked on the balls of her feet. "Do you think you can take a break for dinner?"

"It *is* dinnertime. A man needs to eat," Evangeline pointed out, and Augustus vowed to kill her.

"I *am* taking a break for dinner tonight," he said, firing a sideways glare at his incorrigible sibling. "But as my sister reminded me, I haven't been home to see my mother in four days, and she'll be expecting me."

Carolina's face fell, but she recovered with a big, beaming smile, brighter than all the ones before. "Aw. Well, that's very sweet of you, Augustus. I'm sure your mother appreciates what a loving son you are."

"A perfect gentleman," Evangeline quipped. "Our living proof chivalry marches on."

"You're putting in a lot of hours," Carolina said, ignoring Evangeline altogether. "I hope you're taking breaks."

"When I need them."

"Why, tomorrow he'll be taking a lunch break. You should come by then!" Evangeline suggested.

"Yeah?" Carolina brightened. "Sure, okay. I will." She waved at them both. "See you then!"

As she walked away, Augustus spun on his sister. "What are you trying to do?"

"Get you laid?"

"I'm serious. What's gotten into you?"

"She likes you, Aggie. She always has."

"What are you talking about? I barely know her, except as Colleen's friend."

Evangeline pulled the sign from his hands and set it on an empty file cabinet. "You get all twisted about a pile of insulation where it's not supposed to be, but wouldn't know flirting if it slapped you upside the head. She's loved you for years. Colleen used to think she only came around for a chance at time with you."

Augustus shook his head. "That's crazy."

Evangeline laughed. "I don't know what she sees in you, either!"

Augustus glowered.

"I don't know why you're so bent out of shape. She's short of a few screws, but she's a fox, Aggie. If I hadn't been standing here, she would've bent herself over that desk—"

"Stop. I mean it." He stretched his arms over his head. "Isn't she with Rory Sullivan, anyway?"

"Who knows? Their relationship is more complicated than quantum mechanics. Probably doesn't help that he's still got the hots for Colleen."

Augustus didn't want to think about this anymore. If he politely rebuffed Carolina's continued advances, she'd eventually lose interest. He wouldn't give it another thought.

But he was lost for anything useful after that strange interruption, so he told Evangeline to grab her backpack and get ready to go.

"Nah, I'm gonna beat feet and catch some of my friends at Preservation Hall before the line gets too long."

"I thought you were escorting me to dinner?"

Evangeline heaved her backpack over one shoulder. "I'm sufficiently convinced you'll do the right thing on your own."

It wasn't his place to scold her, or tell her what to do with her life. But he'd heard rumors about the company his sister was keeping... ones he'd kept to himself, lest Charles go ape, as Madeline used to say. It was better to monitor the situation himself and keep it contained.

"Be careful," he said.

"Careful?"

"Yeah. Careful."

"What's that supposed to mean?" she demanded, as she worked to tuck her wild curls into a rubber band. It snapped against the pressure, and she winced and cursed.

"Nothing. I've heard... things, about some of your friends."

"Aggie, come on, I'm not like..." She stopped herself, wearing a mask of horror. She quickly moved closer and squeezed his cheeks between her fingers. "You're the one Mama is worried about. All these hours. Might think about lying and telling her you're with a woman. She'd be a lot less concerned if she didn't know you were sleeping here."

Evangeline skipped off.

CHAPTER 2

A Curse by Any Other Name

The Deschanel Magi Collective Council finished the recitation of the ceremonial vows and Ophelia called the meeting to order.

"Before we explore official business, I wish to welcome our dearest Kitty Guidry to the mystifying world of adulthood," Ophelia said. Her gnarled hand trembled from beneath her red velvet robe as she placed it over Kitty's. "Happy birthday, dear."

"Happy birthday, darling," Pierce said.

Kitty smiled at the old woman. "Thank you, Tante. And you, too, Daddy."

"Well, then." Ophelia settled her hands back into her lap. "We've been fortunate, you know. We live in a period of relative peace for the Deschanels. None of you were alive the last time the Deschanel Curse swept through our ranks. When my brother, Charles, lost three of his children at the turn of the century."

"Why do we have to call it that? The Deschanel Curse? It sounds so archaic," winsome Claudius Broussard asked. Earlier, during vows, Colleen had caught him checking his hair in the reflection of the silver decanter. He'd never met another he couldn't charm, organic or not.

"A curse by any other name is still a curse," said Pierce Guidry.

He knew. He'd heard the stories from their mother, Blanche, before she'd stopped talking about the past. Back when she still came to Council meetings. Cassius, Pierce's half-brother, had experienced a much different childhood than his older half-siblings.

"We don't mince words in here," Ophelia warned the room. "Nor do we suffer fools."

"Sorry, Tante." Cassius looked down.

Colleen had a flash of empathy for her cousin. *Don't feel bad. Not even you can charm the woman who sees all.*

"This family *is* cursed. Your lack of occasion to bear witness does not change the facts," she went on. "We have only two pieces of housekeeping to review, and then we'll discuss the news we've received from France." She turned to Kitty. "Review the ledger, please."

"We have a need for a volunteer this summer. Want me to read the details?"

"Yes, child," Ophelia urged.

"Colleen has performed a ton of organization for the Collective over the past two years, when she's not in class, which has revealed we have a need for far more," Kitty read. She smiled at Colleen. "I know Colleen would say she doesn't need help, but our archives are large, and the organization has helped us locate old files and stories we'd all but given up on."

Kitty was right, Colleen didn't want the help. Buried in curling parchment and the dusty consolation of the old vault, surrounded by the infinite quiet of a place largely untouched by life, was her only comfort. She went from class to the vault, over and over, falling into her bed exhausted at the end of each day. Her brain stayed focused only on these specific things she'd allowed inside. Her mind had always been a series of compartments, and as long as she kept some of them filled, the others stopped calling to her.

"I'll help," Pansy said. "Placide won't let me lift a finger at home now, on account of the baby. He'll be happy to see me fixing after paperwork instead."

The summer prior, Pansy had married a Cajun man from

Breaux Bridge who treated her like a princess. He was twice her age and balked at the money he married into. But Pansy was accustomed to a very specific life, and to hold onto her, he'd grudgingly moved into the mansion she inherited as part of her Deschanel estate entitlement. He drew the line at her notions of doing anything more strenuous than raising their children. Rex, she said. Pansy was quite positive the child was a boy, despite that no tests had even confirmed she was even with child yet, nor had the family healers felt comfortable providing confirmation.

"Thanks, Pansy," she said. It was pointless to turn down the help. Ophelia knew Colleen didn't need it in a practical sense, so she'd decided she needed it for other reasons.

"We'll have ourselves some cousin time! We haven't spent time together since we were kids, Colleen."

"Has it been that long?" Colleen's mind traveled elsewhere. It woke up next to Rory, as she had for night after night this past winter; first feeling as if she was exactly where she was meant to be, and later wishing she could take it all back, even the best parts. It considered increasing—again—her course load so she could start medical school faster and launch herself farther from a childhood that had never made sense to her like the adulthood beckoning in the distance. It regarded the rift between herself and all her siblings, but mostly Evangeline, whose absence had left a gap bigger than she could have ever anticipated. It remembered...

Maddy, I don't think you'll be happy until the world burns around you and you're the goddamn glowing center of it all.

"Colleen? You okay?" Cassius asked.

"Yes, fine. Making mental notes." The rest of the Council had turned to watch her as well. She could smack Cassius for drawing the attention her way. She channeled her focus staying present.

"Kitty?" Ophelia urged.

"Yes, Tante. The other item on the housekeeping list is about family record keeping. We need to collect birth records for all our 1971 and 1972 family babies. We also need to visit any births from the last decade to see if the children have begun to manifest powers yet, and record those in the ledgers as well. I believe it's also time for us to go through and do an overall refresh."

Ophelia nodded. "This will be new for some of you. It's standard practice for us to record all family births, and then schedule regular visits with the families as the children begin to manifest. But we know abilities can change over time as well. Some strengthen, others weaken. Some even manifest later in life, as we've seen, especially in the cases of mystics or elementalists. It's important we always have a very current and accurate register."

"I'll take the lead on this," Pierce offered. "Pansy and Kitty have enough to worry about, and Colleen already has a tall order with organizing the files."

"Thanks, Dad," his two daughters replied in unison.

"Let me know how I can help," Eugenia said.

"Yes, thank you, darling." Ophelia started to say something else, then erupted in a coughing fit. Kitty and Pansy reached over to steady her, but she waved them away. After several excruciating moments, she pulled a silk handkerchief from her pocket and dabbed at her mouth. "As I said earlier, our family is in a period of relative peace. The Curse last struck in 1903, if my memory serves. When my dear nephew, August, passed on in '61, it was of a long-standing disease, and with no others to follow, we have always considered that a tragedy of life, rather than of a supernatural interference. Things were quiet then until the unexpected death of our dear Madeline." She offered Colleen a tight, but warm, smile. "Two years now have passed, and we were very near to calling this one a simple tragedy as well. But now we have been sent notice of the untimely passing of two of our cousins in France. We will share the names, though I doubt they will mean much to any of us."

"Yes, as Tante Ophelia said, there are two. One is a Heloise Deschanel, aged fourteen. She drowned in a lake near her family's home. The other, a Pascal Deschanel, was thirty-nine and had a heart attack, though by all accounts was in perfect health," Kitty read.

"That makes three in a relative short span," Ophelia said. "And three cannot be set aside."

"You didn't see them, Tante?" Pierce asked. "In visions?"

"I don't see everything, child. Only what the visions give me."

"But we aren't ready to say for certain this is Brigitte's Curse, right?" asked Eugenia and Pierce groaned. Eugenia was the second child of Blanche, from Blanche's second marriage, but was the favored child, and the one whose line was set to inherit everything. Her relationship with her older half-brother was not fractured altogether, but they found their strains in the subtlety of power struggles.

"In here, can we *not* play the skeptics? In here, of all places?" Pierce asked.

"In here, of all places, we must," Eugenia said. She cocked her head. "The family looks to us to lead them, in the darkness and the light. They look to us to separate wheat from chaff and to know when it's safe to breathe and when we must worry."

Colleen had always liked Eugenia. She possessed a quiet strength and was level-headed, focused in a thoughtful way. She reminded Colleen of herself, but Eugenia, a decade Colleen's senior and already a mother three times over, had always been just out of her reach for a friendship beyond the kinship of cousins. She was smarter than her brother Pierce, and so much more like her mother, Blanche, which was probably why Blanche had chosen her above both Pierce and Cassius.

Colleen was reminded again how important it was to bring in more from her father's line, to the Council. All three of Blanche's surviving children were Council members. Two of Pierce's daughters. That left Colleen, on an island, set apart from the interfamily dynamics and struggles of her peers in the room. She had grown up with them, but in many of the ways that mattered, she hardly knew them.

"Eugenia is right," Cassius said. "This is why we exist as a Council. This is hard for us because it's new. None of us were alive when this happened before, except Tante Ophelia. We have to trust her guidance on this one, so we can guide the others."

Pierce sighed. "Fine, brother. Tante, when this last happened, at what point did the family begin to believe the Curse was back?"

"At the loss of the third," Ophelia replied. "You are looking to me for something finite and tangible, but we are not dealing with anything of the sort. There is no template for this accursed tether our family wears. Is it not possible that every untimely death is not somehow tied back to Brigitte's vow to see us suffer? How would we know?" She coughed again, and something landed in her handkerchief. She regarded the prize and stuffed the rag back in her pocket. "There is no magic number. There is no guidebook."

"Shouldn't we consider that there might be an explanation grounded in science?" Colleen asked.

A titter of chuckles passed through the room. It echoed through the chamber, which stretched into the darkness.

"Maybe for others, science makes sense," Pansy said. "Ain't never made sense for us."

Colleen ignored her and turned to her great-aunt. "But science has come a long way since the nineteenth century, or even since the start of this century. If we really think there's a correlation between these deaths, and, as Eugenia said, we have a responsibility to the family, shouldn't we at least explore it?"

"And study what?" Pierce asked. "What, exactly, could science tell us? *Science* would tell us your sister died from trauma caused by a horrible accident. That Heloise's lungs filled with water, asphyxiating her. That Pascal's heart gave out, probably because of some undiagnosed heart disease."

"Maybe," Colleen said. "Or maybe it could help us discover something genetic. Something recessive that becomes dominant every couple generations and predisposes us—"

"Enough," Ophelia said. "There are very few things not open for safe debate in this room. That we are cursed is not one of them. Eugenia, I'd like you to please reach out to other branches across Europe and see if there are others we must add to the list."

Eugenia nodded.

Colleen's chest burned at the dismissal. Only Ophelia knew that Colleen's motivation to become a doctor was a desire to understand her family's afflictions and gifts from a scientific lens. And, rather than shutting it down, as she'd just done in front of all of Colleen's peers, she'd encouraged Colleen's dream. Now, she didn't know what to think.

The meeting continued and then came to a close, but Colleen's cheeks were aflame with shame and embarrassment, and her mind couldn't stop weaving further betrayal around her aunt's words.

"Having a sleepover here, are we?"

Colleen looked up. The room around her was empty, except Ophelia. The others had gone home, though she couldn't say when. She had no memory of anything past Ophelia's harsh words.

"Sorry, Tante. I'm leaving." She slid her chair back, but her aunt laid a hand on her forearm.

"You're cross with me."

Colleen started the denials, but there was never any point in deception with the woman who had borne no children of her own but was nonetheless the undisputed family matriarch. "I don't understand. When I told you what I wanted to do, you encouraged me."

"Yes."

"Forgive me, but I really don't—"

"I think you do," Ophelia replied. "I have led this family as best as I know how, Colleen. Often that required a certain degree of rigidity and maintaining of the status quo. People fear what they cannot understand. They rally around those things they do."

"You're saying..." Colleen searched for the words. "I don't know."

"You do. Go on."

"You think they're incapable of action when the answer is nebulous, but when it's clear... even if the prognosis feels hopeless..."

"Yes," Ophelia said. "Something along those lines. Leadership demands much of you, but perhaps the hardest is knowing when to open the window and let others in, and when to close it and protect them."

"Then why tell me this at all?"

"Because, one day, a day that will not be so very far in the future, you'll be sitting in my chair, Colleen. You'll be leading this family, and when you do, you'll have the authority to choose when to open the window and when to close it."

"What? Me?" She'd always assumed it would be Eugenia. Strong, savvy Eugenia with the perfect husband and three perfect young sons. Blanche's darling. Everyone's darling.

"Of course, you. And I can't demand, or even ask, you to lead the family the way I did. When you're magistrate, you can decide if science is the path to take this family down. If they're ready for something they can't wrap their arms around."

"But... Tante, I'm nowhere near ready to step into your shoes." She couldn't bring herself to say the rest, that at ninety-four, this could happen at any time. Colleen would have said it was her greatest fear, before she had buried one of her siblings.

The lines in her great-aunt's face shuffled around as the old woman smiled. "Do you know how I came to be magistrate? Have I ever told you?"

Colleen shook her head.

Ophelia chortled. "I declared myself magistrate, that's how!" Her laugh dissolved into hacking coughs before she continued. "When my grandparents, Charles and Brigitte, brought the family to Louisiana, they did not bring with them the tradition of the Council. The Council goes back centuries. Seventeenth or eighteenth, I forget, and such details become less important over time. Charles' father, my great-grandfather, was magistrate in France, and he beseeched Charles to continue this practice in the New World. I discovered this by accident, as a child, when I overheard my grandfather talking about this very thing to my father. When I was old enough, I wrote a letter to several relatives in France, looking to piece together what the Deschanel Magi Collective was, and how I could continue what my grandfather had failed to do."

Colleen was transfixed. She'd never heard any of this, and she doubted Ophelia had shared these memories with anyone else. She'd known only that the Collective was very old.

"I'm growing very tired, so let me reach my point," Ophelia said. "Our traditions bind us, Colleen. But all traditions begin somewhere. You'll have your time."

"Thank you for telling me this, Tante. I always feel so much better after time with you."

Ophelia settled her cane into the wood floor and wobbled to her feet. "Sleep calls, but there was more I meant to say to you, dear."

Colleen sat back down. "Okay."

"Forgive Evangeline," her aunt said. "She needs you, but you need her more. The grief you all share requires unity to overcome, and you will need unity in the coming years. And this boy... Rory..."

"Yes?"

"Do not lose another hour of sleep over him," Ophelia said. "Rory isn't the man you're going to marry." When Colleen's jaw fell loose, her aunt added, "I'll beg your forgiveness at a later date for my unsolicited soothsaying, but for now, you have more important things to deal with than the fickleness of love that has already expired."

CHAPTER 3

Virgins and Super Freaks

"It's a nice day. You should go outside."

Maureen hurled her math textbook—really, the only book in her room, and only because she had no choice—across the room. It hit the wall with a thud and slid to the floor, pages akimbo.

"I'm just saying."

"No, you're not saying anything, you're dead." Maureen dove under the covers and pulled the blankets tight over her head.

She screamed when Madeline appeared beside her in her fortress. "Look, Maureen, as an empath, I get why seeing your dead loved ones is a drag, but as your sister—"

"No, my sister is dead. Dead!" She pressed her face into the pillow. "Dead, like Peter, like Father!" Dead, dead, dead, all of them, but that didn't stop them from making demands. Madeline begged and pleaded with Maureen to pass messages to her sisters and brothers, to their mother, but Maureen couldn't give her what she wanted. No one could ever know she was a freak who communed with the dead.

She couldn't explain to anyone why she didn't grieve for Madeline as they did. That, for her, Madeline had never actually *left*.

You have to tell Augustus it's not his fault! And Colleen, oh, she'll blame herself forever! And tell Mama...

No, she couldn't, even if it did tear at her heart to say no.

"Why, Maureen?" Peter sang in his melancholy refrain. She'd thought the rules of these... ghosts, or whatever the hell they were, tethered them to certain places only, but apparently not Peter Evers. Peter Evers had evolved, to torture her at home now, too. What else might he evolve to do?

There was no one to ask.

"Sweet Maureen, we're still family, even in the afterlife," her father said.

"Hell's bells!" Was there nothing, nothing at all that could turn this off, once and for all?

Her mother's pistol, perhaps. Maureen didn't know how to use it, but it couldn't be so hard, right? Pull the trigger, boom, problems over.

And not just the problem of these meddlesome ghosts, either.

Madeline knew about Maureen's most recent trauma. Father, too, probably, and maybe even that pervert Peter. Only Madeline had tried to talk to her about it, though.

As if talking did any good at all. Talking wouldn't erase the baby growing in her womb. It wouldn't change the laws, either of the court of society. It certainly wouldn't do anything about her mother's insistence Maureen had no say at all in what happened to the baby, either.

When she'd suggested going away to a convent to have the child and send it off for adoption, like other young and unwed mothers did, Irish Colleen practically fainted away. *Your father left me to protect you children* and *your fortune. You really think it would be wise to have a bastard running around out there who can show up twenty years from now to challenge their right to financial entitlement?*

Pierce Guidry knew a guy, who knew a guy. Maureen had seen the propaganda in her health class about these "guys." Back-alley abortionists who were less concerned with sanitation and more with cash up front. But apparently that was good enough for Mama! The appointment was made. The date set, for when Maureen would be forced against her will to murder her own baby.

Pleading to her mother's Catholic guilt made matters worse. "Don't drag Jesus into this, Maureen. He didn't make these decisions for you. But he did give us science, and doctors who know how to help fix things when our children make terrible mistakes."

"So, Jesus created abortions?"

"He made me your mother, and as your mother I make the rules!"

Okay, sure. Whatever that meant.

The clock downstairs chimed noon. Their appointment with "the guy" was in an hour, somewhere out in Carrollton. They'd ride the St. Charles streetcar to the end of the line, and then walk six blocks. Maureen didn't imagine she'd be real keen on walking those six blocks again after whatever heinous procedure awaited her, but her mother had said the service included a discreet taxi home to Oak Haven.

"I know this is hard, Maureen. There's still a way out of this, you know."

Maureen pinched off the flutter of emotion in her chest. She channeled the emotion into anger. "Oh yeah, Maddy? What's that? Die like you?"

"I'd never wish death on you," her dead sister answered, smiling sadly. "But you could leave. As long as you're here, Mama will make decisions for you. You have no choice. Out there..."

"Out *there* is *nothing*!" Maureen cried, for her world was never as big as Madeline imagined hers to be, and even the mere thought of it being so was enough to send her spiraling into hopelessness.

HER FRIEND SUSAN SHOWED HER THE PRINTING PRESS IN the office of the school newspaper. They had two, actually; the big one was for the weekly Sacred Heart Gazette. The other was for smaller projects, like the fliers plastered on the boards by the front office, or outside the gymnasium, announcing school dances, fundraisers, sports sign-ups, and the other events of the high school social calendar.

Maureen had, briefly, an inkling to be a school journalist. She even went as far as taking one of their fliers once. But she'd transferred from public school to the Academy of the Sacred Heart when she left middle school behind, and all the key positions in clubs and sports were taken by the girls who'd been Sacred Heart students since kindergarten.

Susan was one of those girls, but she was more approachable and friendlier than most of them. Maureen thought this was because Susan was a bit simple in the head, but she was nice enough and Maureen had nothing against a simple girl. Simple girls made easy wives later. Easy wives, easy lives. Everyone knew that.

She was the closest thing Maureen had to a friend, unless she counted Chelsea Sullivan, and she only counted her occasionally, depending on whether they were embroiled in one of their epic fights, which they were the day Maureen found herself in the office of the school newspaper. Chelsea wouldn't have approved of the idea that blossomed from the visit, at least not outwardly. She wanted everyone to think she was as pristine as her three older brothers, but she wasn't, and Maureen reminded her of that a little too often.

Susan wasn't on the newspaper staff. She was responsible for collecting all the discarded newspapers each week and putting them in a bin to be picked up and taken to the transfer station for paper recycling downtown.

"Anyone can use the smaller press, but you need a key to open the cover for the big one," Susan said, eyes wide, as if the idea of using a key was almost too much to comprehend. "Groovy, huh?"

"Yeah. I suppose." It wasn't groovy at all, actually, but it did help pull an idea mulling around in Maureen's head into a way forward.

Susan lifted the cart full of discarded papers. "Okay, this thing is full now. Let's go."

"I'll catch up to you," Maureen lied.

Simple Susan didn't ask why Maureen wanted to hang out behind with the printing presses. She just flashed her toothy grin and skipped off with a groan as the cart wheels strained against the weight. "See ya!"

The size of the smaller press didn't make it simpler to operate. Susan's quick demonstration was enough to get Maureen in business in under an hour, though, and by then, all the kids had gone home. She hoped the same held true for the public high school ten minutes away, up on Claiborne.

She found the school mostly empty. A few scattered kids rushed to finish their tasks and get home. Those lone stragglers had a ruddy, dangerous look to them, in their contemporary clothes that contrasted to the wholesome and sterile uniforms of the private schools. One boy had burnt orange bell-bottoms and side-burns so long he could almost tie them under his chin. Another, a leather jacket and a cigarette tucked behind his ear, against his greasy blond hair.

They regarded her with the same look she trained back on them: foreigner. Intruder. But they said nothing, and so she went on her way.

This was a world she didn't miss, but craved, the way her mother often had a hankering for peanut butter cookies.

Maureen found the boys' locker room with relative ease. She looked both ways before slipping inside. The coast was clear here, too, and so she went about her work quickly, but with less fear of being discovered.

VIRGINS ONLY SECRET CLUB. This, the most important part of her whole message, was as big as the press could print. The rest of the details were smaller, so only those most interested would bother to read. *SEARCY'S BOATHOUSE ON TCHOUPITOULAS. CUM STRAIT THERE TUES AND THURS AFTER FINAL BELL BUT ONLY IF UR SERYUS ABOUT HAVING UR MIND BLOWN. THE PLACE IS ABANDINNED. BRING BEER AND SUMTHING 2 LAY ON.*

That was on Monday, and she wasn't really expecting anything on the first Tuesday following her propaganda campaign. So when five boys showed up, her heartrate exploded into a thousand tiny stars before her eyes. Could she do this? She wanted to. She really wanted to. She *needed* to. She could accept Peter was a pervert who had used her, but she wasn't content to leave it at that.

There was Calvin Abernathy, Greer Baldwin, and James Grant, all freshmen. Oscar Messick was a sophomore, and Owen Oakes a senior. All but Greer were nice-looking. She might have to pretend with him, but she was good at that from her experience with Peter, who was quite average—or had been, before Charles killed him. James she'd actually had a crush on since last year, and just before she made her speech, she thought to herself how things had a funny way of working out.

"You all know why you're here?"

Nervous nods were her reply. Shuffling of feet. A few titters. Probably wondering if this was a trick, or the best thing that would ever happen.

Maureen stepped up on an old metal husk, some forgotten piece of machinery. "Do you solemnly swear you are all virgins?"

Variations of yes, and yeah, and even an m-hmm sounded in the abandoned warehouse.

"And you've each brought a hundred dollars?" Her hands splayed against her hips. "Put it over there, on that bench. I want to see it first."

The five boys each dug into their pockets and backpacks, for money they'd gotten from who knows where. These were Uptown boys, who didn't want for much, but it was unlikely their parents had just handed that much cash over, especially if they'd known what it was for.

"Swell," Maureen said. Five hundred dollars! More than some made in a month... and this was only day one. Not that she was doing this for the money, but it would help. There were things Maureen needed to prepare herself to be an ideal future wife—charm school, a wardrobe suitable for someone older and more ready to raise a family—and so she'd simply have to fend for herself. She couldn't wait for her trust to become available in a few years. By then, she'd be an old maid. "Who wants to go first?"

She realized in that moment that she wasn't nervous at all. Not even a little. With Peter, she'd fumbled through the motions, desperate to be good enough, to not be a simpleton in the face of his great experience. Here, she was the queen, the one who knew her way around the bedroom. She was in charge.

They all exchanged uncomfortable glances. Oscar, finally, stepped forward. Maureen pointed to the blanket. He looked back at the other guys, with a question in his eyes.

"Never mind them. They can watch," she said, for no other reason than she wanted them to feel the authority she wielded. To never forget it.

Oscar lowered himself to the blanket. He sat, awkwardly, awaiting instruction.

"Well, take them off!" she commanded. "Hell's bells!"

His pants shuffled off; his excitement at the moment stood at full attention. He didn't want the others to see, she knew that, but that was part of the thrill, and so was the next part.

Maureen wiggled her panties off and shimmied them to the floor. She stepped out of the pool of white cotton and slid her skirt up and over her waist. When she fell to her knees in front of him, she could see how hard he was breathing. His erection bounced with his heaving pants.

She placed herself over him and pulled him inside her, with a disinterested look that she hoped conveyed she'd done this so many times it was nothing at all. He shivered and cried out at the sudden burst of pleasure, and somewhere, beyond, the other boys groaned as well. Yes. This. Now, this was hers. Not Peter's. Hers.

Why, Maureen?

"Because I can," she whispered.

Not quite an hour later, all five had gotten what they came for, and Maureen had never, not once in all her life, felt more alive, more in control. Only the soreness between her legs and the distant pang in her chest warned her otherwise.

The schools had of course gotten wind of the fliers and kept a vigilant watch over the locker rooms, but by then, word had gotten around and she was easily able to communicate the changes in locations by word-of-mouth alone.

For two months, Maureen lorded over the young men of the different high schools she'd plastered fliers in, making men of boys, and with each capture of virginity, breathing a new life into herself. One that no one, not Peter, not the ghosts ruining her life, not her mother, not anyone could take from her.

And it was all perfect bliss until the morning sickness started.

"Why, Maureen?" Peter's sad eyes followed her as she changed into the shapeless smock her mother placed in her closet for the terrible event.

"Did you know I shagged two dozen of the boys you taught Shakespeare to, Peter?" Maureen chirped with a sugary smile.

"Why, Maureen?"

"Charles was right to kill you. You're such a terrible bore," Maureen accused. "A hack in the sack, too."

The tears started without warning.

Was she really in control, ever? Ever? Not long after the first of her Virgins Only Secret Club meetings she'd started to hear the rumors about the little Uptown prostitute. She wanted to scream in defense of herself, but then she realized that's exactly what she'd been doing. Selling sex for money. Almost five thousand dollars was rolled up in her sock drawer as evidence. An unthinkable amount of money for someone her age. For anyone, of any age.

And now one of those four dozen boys-to-men was the father of her child. There would never be any way to know which one, even if she had the child.

"You have more than enough money to get out of here, Maureen. You have more than what the average adult makes in a year. You are so much better off than you think," Madeline said, and she was crying, too. Was it really crying when the crier was a ghost? Maureen didn't know. She'd never know.

"And do what?"

"Anything! But you'd have your baby. And time to figure things out," Madeline pleaded.

"I'm not like you, Maddy." For the first time, the words weren't an indictment. A small part of Maureen wished she *was* like Madeline, free to roam the world aimlessly, without thought to her future. But Maureen had always known what her future would be, and though it gutted her to follow her mother's demands, she was practical enough to understand she would not find a husband with a child born without a father. "I'm just not."

"You can't go back from here," Madeline said. "If I believed this is what *you* wanted, I would support you, but I know you don't... I know in your heart—"

"Whatever heart I might have had was ripped out and ground into meat years ago."

"I know you feel alone, but you're not. I promise, you're not."

Maureen sniffled, laughed. "You mean you? I have you? My dead sister?"

"Not just me, but yes, if whatever gift you've been given allows me to stay, I'll stay. I want to help you. You don't know what it's like to have regrets you can't fix... if I can help you, I'll do anything it takes."

Maureen pulled the silk headscarf over her hair and tied it. "Well, you can't. No one can."

"Why, Maureen?" wailed Peter from the corner.

Madeline lowered her head and sighed. "I was never a very good Catholic, Maureen, but I know you still believe in God, so I'll be praying for you."

ELIZABETH'S FEET DANGLED OVER THE LINOLEUM FLOOR. She wasn't quite tall enough for her feet to reach, though she'd spent enough time in the vice principal's office to attempt several different positions, sliding up and down, to see if that made the difference.

It didn't, but most of the other kids she saw in and out of the back room of shame had the same problem. She suspected the height of the chairs was intentional, to remind them they were still just children and that someone else was in charge.

She hated this chair. This vice principal. This school. Somehow, this school turned out to be the worst one of all, and after her last episode, she didn't think she'd be here much longer. This should feel like relief, but instead she had only the undying pit of dread growing in her stomach. This was her... fifth school? Sixth? She'd lost count, but she knew her mother was running out of options for places to send her when this one inevitably told them they could no longer handle Elizabeth Deschanel's antics.

Elizabeth couldn't handle them, either, and that was the problem. She wished she could be literally anyone else. Anyone else in the world, even the starving child in Africa her mother threatened to send her uneaten food to, because even they had flashes of peace. Moments of clarity. Elizabeth lived in a world that perpetually showed her how bad things could be, and then she was forced to watch as these bad things came to pass. Every hour of every day.

Her father called what each of his children had gifts. But this was not a gift. It was a curse.

She would've thought she would have learned to keep her mouth shut by now. Sharing her visions had never led to anything good. Bullying, cruel notes in her locker, suspensions, expulsions. But sharing what she'd seen was the only relief Elizabeth could ever find. When she told others what she'd seen, it was more than sharing, it was an unburdening of sorts, where she transferred some of that pain out into the world. It was the only way she knew how to survive, but each and every time her world grew more strained and less available.

Today, the vision had sent her to her knees. Eleven little ones at the Montessori down the road would lose their short lives in a terrible school fire. Her classmates had first yelled at her, and then some came in with tears, for they had siblings in the school. And by the time the teacher cut through the mess of children clawing at Elizabeth for her words, the fire trucks were racing by; the damage done.

Her lip was bloody and the bruises over her body ached, but she couldn't say a word about it. She couldn't risk Charles hearing and doing something else he couldn't take back.

Elizabeth watched as parents came and picked up the children whose siblings had lost their battle that day... the haggard, accusing looks from both parent and child thrown in her direction. But she hadn't caused it! She'd even tried to stop it!

Which was pointless, anyway, because there was no changing the future.

One by one they left with their parents, until it was only Elizabeth, hunkered over in the chair that was too tall for anyone, too exhausted for the tears she wanted to cry.

The creak and swish of the office doors opening piqued her attention. She looked up to see Connor Sullivan shuffling her way.

"Hey, Lizzy." He jumped up onto one of the chairs, missed, and hopped forward on one foot to regain his balance. He made it the second time, but his cheeks were flushed. He pressed his dark hair out of his eyes, blowing madly when he failed at that, too.

"What are you doing here?"

He lifted his shoulders. "I snuck out."

"Why?"

"So you wouldn't have to be in the dungeon alone."

The dungeon. That was Elizabeth's name for the dark holding area for all the bad students in need of discipline. Connor knew this because she'd told him. He was her only friend. Not just at present, but ever. He was the only good thing that had come from being transferred to this school, but that would soon be over, as everything was.

"You didn't have to do that."

"I know."

"Mrs. Perkins will *murder* you if she finds you've run off to see me."

Connor grinned. "I know."

That was the thing about Connor. He was a good kid and mostly played by the rules, but he had a twinkle of mischief he reserved for the occasional mild, low-grade anarchy. She hadn't yet seen his future, but she suspected it would involve some mid-level office job and the occasional speeding ticket.

Elizabeth shoved her hands deeper into the crevasse between her knees. "Well, thanks."

"Where's Caldwell? He ever gonna call you back into his office?"

She sighed. "Probably went home. Forgot about me. Wouldn't be the first time."

"I'll call down to Galatoire's and have them bring us supper."

Elizabeth couldn't help but smile. Connor was an odd kid, but so was she, and that made him the only person suitable to share her secrets with. And she had. Some of them, anyway.

"Just no duck, please."

Connor clutched his chest. His green eyes sparkled. "Do you take me for a heathen, madam?"

"I really do think Caldwell forgot about me," Elizabeth said. "Which means he forgot to call my mother, too."

"Are you gonna sleep over, or just give up and go home?"

"What do *you* think I should do?"

"Join the circus," he said without hesitation.

Elizabeth nodded. "Ah, yes. The circus. My talents would be better suited in the Big Top than middle school, that's for sure."

"Elizabeth, Sensational Soothsayer Extraordinaire!" Connor cried, sweeping his arm across the imaginary marquee.

"Or Super Freak." In her head, she started to hum a song by Rick James that wouldn't come out until 1981. *Great. This again.*

"How does that song go again?"

"You're not supposed to know about it, and I'm sorry I ever told you!"

Connor laughed and smacked his hands on his knees. “Forget songs, Lizzy, we need to know what stocks to invest in so we can be independently wealthy and live off our earnings.”

She started to tell him that wasn’t how this worked, she couldn’t choose what to see and not see, and besides it was dishonest, but something in his words sparked a desire in her that had been brewing for years. “If I had the money… I’d run away.”

“Like actually run away, or just camp in the backyard until things blow over?”

“Actually run away.”

Connor frowned, nodding. “Okay, but we need a plan. We can’t just eat out of dumpsters and curl up on discarded mattresses. My mother has a nice tent, but we need supplies, and—”

“I’m not joking!” Elizabeth exclaimed, and the sting of tears that would never fall returned. The last of her tears dried up when she’d first predicted the death of her sister and then watched the eventuality and actuality of the terrible news tear through her family like a relentless cancer.

His face changed. “Yeah, I know you’re not. But if you run away, Elizabeth Deschanel, I’m going with you, and so we need a plan.”

CHAPTER 4

The Odd Bird

Colin had chosen Antoine's for the occasion. It wasn't really an occasion, as far as Charles was concerned, and as far as most of society was probably concerned. A "year-and-a-half" anniversary didn't exist, and was far too imaginative for Colin Sullivan to come up with on his own, that was for damn sure. But Cat wasn't the type of fanciful chick to demand silly things, either, so the idea must have come from somewhere else.

But Charles would have taken Cat to Antoine's every night of the year if she wanted. He wouldn't need occasion to spoil her; to see her soft, pretty face illuminated in a smile, night after night after night. To know he was the cause.

He'd been so raptly listening to Cat's entertaining story about how the mice had escaped the lab in her class earlier that he'd completely forgotten his own date. Jessica, and he only remembered her name this time because Colin had repeated it in his ear a hundred times on the drive to collect the women. *I can't stomach another double date with you botching your date's name, Charles. Especially not tonight.*

It wasn't his fault, really, that he couldn't remember. He never brought the same one twice, and there was only so much useless information a brain could retain. There was science behind that, he was quite certain, but wasn't willing to weather Evangeline's knowing smile by asking.

"How did you catch them?" Jessica leaned forward on her elbows, her thin, braceleted arms wound together. If there was anyone enjoying this story more than Charles, it was probably her.

Cat sipped her wine and laughed. "We didn't."

Jessica's mouth and eyes widened in tandem, scandalized. The glitter from her eyeshadow twinkled under the chandelier. "They probably ran off to start their own little mice families. Do you think so? I do."

Charles shot a hard look at Colin, who replied with an imperceptible shrug and twitch of the head. Colin had chosen this one, and Charles would be damned if that fact wouldn't be continuously pointed out throughout the evening, every time she said something that all but guaranteed Charles wouldn't have sex with her later.

"I don't know," Cat said pleasantly. "I hadn't thought about it, but that's a nice idea."

If any one of Charles' male friends had suggested runaway mice had run off to start a happy family, he would've smacked them upside the head and told them to go home and think about shit, real hard, before they opened their mouth again. As it was, he had to bite his tongue with his date.

But then, there was Cat, always, to remind him there were other virtues than anger and annoyance.

Still, he was annoyed.

Annoyed this date wasn't pretty enough to cancel out her stupidity.

Annoyed this meant he wasn't getting laid later.

Annoyed at this silly year-and-a-half anniversary.

Annoyed it was Colin, and not Charles, going home with Cat tonight.

Even if he put his own confused feelings aside, he struggled to understand the attraction between his best friend and Catherine Connelly. Colin was settled, solid and predictable, while Cat led with her heart. She did well in school, but didn't see the same point in it that Colin did, and would have been equally happy aimlessly roaming the world. Colin had panic attacks if his routine was disrupted, but Cat always suggested they go off script and try something spontaneous, like two weekends ago when she'd dragged him to Destin and made him camp out on the beach, under the stars. She'd been glowing when they returned, and Colin, smiling, nonetheless looked as if he'd been dragged through the outer bands of a Category 5 hurricane.

Yet here they were, a year-and-a-half later. And here Charles was, the third wheel, paired with yet another date he'd forget in a day.

Charles told himself it didn't matter. Irish Colleen had her mind set on marrying him off soon, and it was unlikely he'd have any choice in the whole affair. She probably had the woman picked out already. Every day he went home, his muscles twisted in apprehension, prepared for her to pounce and deliver the inevitable news.

Whoever Charles married, she would be nothing like Cat *or* Jessica. Pliant, fertile, and rich were the only qualifications his mother would worry herself with. The other six could marry for love, but not him. And if not him, then why not Colin? His best friend, who had stuck by him through his endless stream of crimes and mishaps? He might get angry with Charles, but he never left.

"So, Charles, what are you doing with yourself these days?" Cat asked.

Now that you've been kicked out of college again and half the establishments in town to boot, she had the kindness not to add.

"Yes, Charles, what have you been doing with yourself?" Colin asked, with a grin Charles wanted to smack right off his face.

"Helping out with the family, mainly."

Although he'd been avoiding his family at all costs, it wasn't a total lie. After the business with Maureen and that pervy teacher, and then the loss of Madeline—*Look at our mother! Look at that gray! That's you, Maddy! You! You stupid, ungrateful bitch, you are sending our mother to an early grave!*—Charles had made it his sole business to look after his sisters, whether they liked it or not. Elizabeth was in trouble again, and Evangeline was up to something… he just wasn't certain *what*, yet.

"You're such a family man," Cat said, and she gifted him with an adoring smile that sent soft pains to his chest. "You're so lucky to have a big family. Being an only child can be so lonely."

"It sounds incredible to me," Colin said. "I wouldn't have had to share my toys growing up, or my clothes."

She laughed and nudged him. "You have no imagination, Olly."

Charles suppressed a laugh. Colin *hated* being called Olly, but he'd never breathe a word of that to Cat. He might lack imagination, but he was sensitive, far more than he'd ever let on.

"Yeah, Olly," Charles said, and it was completely, totally revenge for the Jessica incident.

Colin shook his head. "I only meant… I have a big family, not just my immediate one, either. The Sullivans are a big lot. I've always wondered what it would be like to just have peace and quiet."

"Of course," Cat said and kissed his cheek. "But that won't stop *us* from having twelve children, right?"

Colin coughed out a laugh.

Charles downed his wine. Twelve children. That would take a lot of sex. He knew they were sleeping together—hell, that Cat was Colin's first—but something about the organic permanence of children made that far more real.

"I think I'll adopt," Jessica said with a dreamy look. "I don't like the idea of a human blooming from my passion flower."

"Your passion flower?" Cat asked.

Jessica blushed. "You know."

"No, I…" Catherine paused. "Oh."

"You know, you could just say you don't want to shit a baby out of your pussy, and we would've all gotten it on the first try," Charles said and signaled for more wine.

Colin set his lips tight. He looked more scandalized than usual, which was an incredible feat. Score another for Charles. "Charles. We're at a nice restaurant."

"Well? Am I wrong?"

Cat hid a smile in her wine glass. She set it down and looked at Jessica. "A lot of women adopt. I think it's an admirable charge, and there are a lot of babies out there who need homes."

"Mice babies, even," Charles said.

Colin kicked him under the table.

"Yes," Cat agreed, and this time she couldn't hide the smile so easily. "Even mice babies."

Charles tipped his glass at Cat. "The good news is, we know where you can find a few."

CHARLES WAS DRUNK ENOUGH THAT BY THE TIME COLIN raised his glass in toast, Charles no longer cared so much about the lovey-dovey bullshit being passed around the table. Blah fucking blah, happy anniversary. Go fuck yourselves.

Their celebratory kiss was lingering, even a little sloppy. Charles could have, would have, kissed her so much better… and more. He'd bet Colin had never even made her come, with his lack of imagination.

After, when they'd dropped off the girls, and Colin drove Charles back home, Colin remarked that the night had gone fairly well. He said it as if he was surprised.

"Yeah, pretty fucking well for a made-up anniversary."

Colin tightened his hands over the steering wheel. "You've never been in a relationship, Charles. You wouldn't understand."

"You're right, Olly. I wouldn't."

"Stop."

Charles threw his hands up. "Where did you even get that idea? The Sears catalog?"

Colin's face recoiled. "The what? No… that doesn't even… I got it from Rory, actually. He used it to win Colleen back, and I guess it worked. She was really touched."

"He's not fucking her again, is he?"

"I don't think so," Colin said. "I mean, not at present."

"At present? What does that mean? Like at this very moment? Are you Superman? Do you have X-ray vision?"

Colin breathed out, a heavy sound. "You're drunk, Charles."

"Very. Now tell me what you meant!"

Colin shrugged his shoulders, but his hands never left the wheel; always the responsible one. Never off his game. "I don't know! I just know they were back together for a little while this winter, but as far as I know, Colleen told him to split again."

Charles laughed. That sounded like Colleen. He pitied the man who eventually married her. That was, if she didn't die a miserable old maid.

But she was still his sister, and a part of him had liked the idea of her with Rory Sullivan, who was, if nothing else, stable and from a good family.

"You seem upset by that." Colin laughed. "Really? After you chased Rory out of your house, how many times?"

"It's my job."

"Your job? To harass your sisters' boyfriends?"

"Don't lie to me and say you've never scared off one of Chelsea's boyfriends."

Colin flicked his turn signal and eased the car onto Third Street. The ride changed from the concrete of St. Charles to the uneven bumps of the cobblestones and brick of the Garden District. "Chels is responsible. She doesn't date."

Charles laughed so hard his stomach seized. He belched up a mix of vomit and red wine. "She's sixteen! *Everyone* is fucking at sixteen, brother. Everyone."

"I wasn't."

Charles' laughter faded. Something burned behind his eyes. No, Colin wasn't then, but he was now. And all those years of restraint had been worth the wait, because now he was sleeping with the kindest, most beautiful woman in the world. A gift Colin deserved, and Charles never would.

"Let me out here," Charles barked.

"What? It's pouring rain!"

Charles threw the door open and made as if he was going to jump out.

"Jesus, Charles, what are you doing?" He slammed on the brakes and the car came to a sliding halt halfway into the intersection. "Okay, okay. Fine. What's gotten into you, anyway?"

"Happy Half-Anniversary," Charles muttered and stumbled off, drunk and sobbing, into the rain and darkness.

EVANGELINE TOSSED BACK THE SHOT OF TEQUILA. SHE winced and started to declare how *awful* it tasted when one of the others shoved a lemon in her mouth.

She spat it out. "That doesn't help."

"Sure it does!" Delia exclaimed, swinging the bottle around. "It neutralizes the taste!"

"No," Evangeline said. "Tequila and lemons are both acidic. You can't neutralize an acid with another acid. What you meant to buy are limes, which are acidic when in their natural state, but become alkaline when ingested by the body."

"Huh?"

"Nothing. Never mind."

Evangeline thought her brain might explode from the grating tambourines and synthesizers of the music they called disco. It wasn't music at all, as far as she was concerned, but she was no judge of such things, and so she said nothing. Whenever she *did* voice an opinion on popular culture, her words were often the catalyst for widening the chasm between normalcy and weirdness.

What was worse, these were kids who were supposed to "get it." She'd found the ad in the paper, small and shoved in the corner of the Classifieds. ASTRONOMY CLUB. COME SEE THE STARS. That sounded incredible, even if she hadn't been actively in search of excuses for taking time off before college. They met twice a week, at the handful of observatories in Orleans Parish, at 10:00 p.m. sharp.

What hadn't been mentioned in the ad was that thirty minutes later, their interest shifted from planetary study to hard-core partying, running far past the hours the bars closed. Their energies flowed sometimes into sunrise, with Ethan's flat in the French Quarter providing the perfect venue.

Evangeline had little interest in partying, especially with her keen understanding of what alcohol did to the brain while intoxicated, but she hadn't known how badly she craved friends until she saw the promise of them dangling before her, at the end of a decision. She suspected they weren't *really* the fans of astronomy that she was—she later learned it was a way of procuring college credit without doing much actual work—but maybe that didn't matter.

At first, she'd told herself the ingestion of alcohol was for scientific reasons. It was one thing to understand something intellectually, and another to experience in a practical setting, and this gave her the perfect laboratory. But as time went on, she ran out of excuses, and the only one left was the truth: when drinking... when stoned out of her mind... she could forget the rest. Colleen. Madeline.

Madeline. Screaming and crying.

Madeline. Scared and alone.

Madeline. In the bus stop at the edge of town, in the middle of the night.

Only Augustus understood, even if there was an unspoken agreement between them never to speak the words aloud. But she felt their shared agony in the spaces between the work they did together, quietly, channeling their focus into results.

He wasn't the reason she'd taken the year off school. Or he was, but he wasn't the only reason. There were many, and like the great Theory of Gestalt, when placed together they were so much more malignant than the sum of their parts.

Craig handed her a beer. "I don't like that liquid fire either," he said and flopped beside her on the oversized purple couch. The thing smelled like piss, booze, and something more human, more feral, but no one seemed to mind.

Evangeline accepted the drink. She tucked her thick, wild hair behind her ears, but it was no use. It was never any use. She may as well be Medusa. "Thanks."

"It's copacetic," he said and pinched the neck of the bottle between his thumb and forefinger. Took a swig. "You seemed really into the stars tonight."

"I'm always really into it."

"Yeah," he said. "I've noticed."

"You have?"

Craig nodded. He kicked off his shoes, which seemed to shoot out of nowhere from under his ridiculous bell bottoms. "I've figured out you're not here for the college credits."

Evangeline sipped her beer. "I think I'm the only one."

"Nah, don't be embarrassed, doll. It's groovy."

"Really?"

"I totally dig smart chicks."

She heard someone fiddling with the record player behind her. The music switched to the one sound she hated more than disco: Joan Baez. Evangeline groaned.

"Wanna dance?" Craig asked.

Evangeline snorted. "To this shit?"

Craig threw his head back and laughed. His glasses toppled over his forehead and landed on the floor, which he didn't seem to notice, though Evangeline couldn't stop thinking about it and wondering when he would have the presence of mind to retrieve them.

"You're an odd bird, Evangeline," Craig said with a strange smile, but it was his eyes she noticed more, which held a hint of fun but also something more seductive and serious.

"I try," she replied, growing nervous without understanding why.

Craig's arm appeared behind her shoulder, and when she turned to look, to evaluate what had shifted between them, he shoved his tongue in her mouth and twirled it around, in something resembling a kiss.

He was a terrible kisser, not that she had much experience in such things with which to make comparison.

"The bedroom is open," Craig said.

"I'm a virgin," Evangeline replied. She didn't know how to flirt, or if she even wanted to.

"Yeah?" Craig kissed her again, transferring a mouthful of beer he'd seemingly forgotten to swallow. "I can fix that."

EVANGELINE DRAPED HER BOOTS OVER ONE ARM AS SHE stumbled down Royal, toward Canal. She could hardly see her way through the tears, which were inexplicable to her, for she had caused her own discordance. She had followed Craig to the bedroom, let him undress her, standing stiffly while he first shoved his fingers inside her and then, pressed on her back atop the scratchy afghan, the rest of him.

She was too exhausted, too empty, to even make a clinical observation of the act. She knew, though, that she hadn't enjoyed it. That, in her inexperience, she hadn't known she was supposed to clean herself up after and now felt what was left of the evening running down her left leg, which was why she couldn't make herself put on her treasured boots. She couldn't ruin those, too, like she'd ruined so much else.

There was blood, too. Of course there was. She'd known that would happen.

Evangeline had stolen a zip tie on her way out the door. For some reason, there'd been a whole bunch of them wound together on a table, without explanation. So she'd helped herself, wrapping the hard plastic around her dark mane. She hardly needed to tighten it at all, and it wouldn't last, but it only needed to get her home.

Maybe she should have left. Gone far, far away to college, where she could lose herself in theory, where emotion was counter to science, and had no place.

Colleen would know what to do. She was the bridge between those worlds, always had been. But there would be no late night sessions with her sister, where advice and love would be dispensed in equal measure. Maybe never again, either.

But Augustus needed her. He needed her, even if he could never say the words, and Evangeline would hold on to that meaning with every last fiber, until there was nothing of herself left to give.

CHAPTER 5
Everything is Changing

Colleen successfully kept her thoughts at bay the remainder of spring, and as the season began to shift, from humid breezes to subtropical swelter, she felt content in having accomplished much while thinking of little.

She hadn't exactly ignored Ophelia's words. They were there, in the wings, awaiting consideration. *Forgive Evangeline.* Well, she had, but forgetting was something altogether, and forgetting would first require thinking, and a level of emotional focus Colleen couldn't spend on anyone or anything. It was far from selfless, far from who she was before and still wanted to be, but it was safe. It was a form of living, even if not an altogether healthy one. Mostly, it was surviving.

And Rory. *Do not lose another hour of sleep over it. Rory isn't the man you're going to marry.* Colleen had guessed as much, less because the union didn't make sense and more that it *did*. Colleen Deschanel and Rory Sullivan... it was hard to imagine two people who fit together better, if one reviewed the sum of their parts on paper. Their esteemed families, their shared focus and commitment to family. Rory, with his beautiful raven hair and green eyes, like all the Sullivan men, and Colleen, with her soft brown tresses and high, contoured features. Their eventual marriage had even been hinted at in the Tattler, and the more esteemed gossip rag of New Orleans Uptown, Moonlight & Magnolia, even outright suggested that invites were imminent. *On Again, Off Again Sullivan Spare and Deschanel Debutante Secret Winter Trysts Revealed.*

He'd even called her about the articles. "Colleen, we need to either put this gossip to rest or stop hurting each other and just be together. I love you. I'll always love you, no matter what we decide." She hadn't missed the slight uptick at the end of the sentence; his voice cracking, hopeful.

"Carolina can give you what I can't."

"Carolina? You know it isn't the same with her… I care for her, but it just isn't the same as it is with us. You know that."

"With Carolina you'll have stability. She'd do anything for you."

A long pause permeated his end of the line. "So, that's it? After everything? You don't even want to try?"

I want to… despite Ophelia's outlook that trying would lead to nothing in the end… despite it all. I love you, too, Rory. I love you and it's hard to imagine ever loving anyone again, to these same depths. Maybe I'll die alone. But to love you means exposing more of the compartments where the bad things are. Where my thoughts come to strangle me. "I can't."

He was crying on the other end. "Colleen, I can't go back and forth like this anymore. It hurts too damn much. If this is it, then this is it, and I won't keep coming back and trying to change your mind. Just tell me… tell me I'm not *wrong*, that you're just afraid to ask someone else to be strong for you. Or with you. I can handle anything, except my heart in limbo."

You're not wrong. You're not wrong, Rory. "I'm sorry, but you're wrong. I'll always hold our time together with fondness, but that season is past us now."

"You don't even sound like yourself."

"Maybe because I'm telling you what you don't want to accept, but need to."

Summer would be tougher to perfect her avoidance skills. She'd signed up for classes, of course, but there were so few of the ones she needed that were offered in what was effectively the off-season, and so she had to settle for two, instead of her usual six—already more than most students. She'd hoped to fill the spare time with more alone time in the vault, but now that Pansy had confirmed she was *not* pregnant, Placide had agreed to let her spend all summer assisting Colleen.

She'd need to find something else; some other place, or activity, or escape. A place where Madeline's death—*I don't think you'll be happy until the world burns around you and you're the goddamn glowing center of it all*—wasn't real, and her love for Rory had never existed. Where Evangeline was just another ship passing in the night.

These thoughts consumed her, dancing on the surface of the compartments protecting the thoughts she could not, would not, access. She hardly recognized herself anymore. Focus had always been part and parcel of who she was, but not escape. She was a leader, not a golem, lurking in the shadows, skittering from corner to corner to avoid anything real.

It had worked for a year and a half. She never expected it to last forever, but an hour longer, a day longer, anything was a relief, and a way to heal, deep down, so she could be whole again. Someday.

Augustus, of all people—the last person she expected—was the one to shatter her good run.

"We need to talk," he said. He appeared in her doorway without knocking, and already she knew it was nothing good.

Colleen suspected nothing about her face suggested she was open for talking, but he either missed that or wasn't concerned by it, because he closed the door behind him and stood at the end of her bed, arms crossed.

"Everything okay?" she asked, though she didn't want to know.

"No, it isn't." He dropped his arms at his sides. His hands twitched, fidgeting as if searching for usefulness and finding only discomfiture. "You need to work things out with Evangeline."

"Do I?" Colleen laughed. The old Colleen wouldn't have, and

she liked that Colleen better, but she was gone at the moment. On holiday. Out to lunch. Insert euphemism here.

He frowned. There was more than concern there; judgment lurked in the gesture. "What's the matter with you?"

She pointed at the book splayed before her on the bed. "At the moment, physics."

"Don't you want to know why I'm here?"

"I suppose you're going to tell me either way."

Augustus grumbled something under his breath. He slumped against her desk chair. "Evangeline has gotten herself into some trouble."

"So, talk to her. Aren't you two working together?"

"If I try to say something, she's going to bolt, and that will only make things worse. She might not come back and... I feel better knowing she's there, where I can keep an eye on her at least some of the time." His face knitted into a deeper frown. "You didn't ask me what trouble she's in."

"Okay, Aggie." Colleen closed the textbook. "What trouble is she in?"

"Have you even asked yourself why she didn't go straight to college?"

No, Colleen didn't want to go there. *All* their escapes rested upon the same, shaky foundation. For that matter, she was more than surprised to see Augustus, who had easily withdrawn the most after the... incident, trying to open up about that very thing. "Tell me about the trouble."

"That's the thing. I don't exactly know."

"Then why are you here?"

"Colleen, Jesus. You're not yourself."

Not the first time someone she loved had said those words.

"So, Evangeline?"

He stood up straight. "She has this group of friends. I've heard some things that make me uncomfortable. She met them through some astronomy club, but they spend more time partying than looking at stars. One of them is a prolific drug dealer. The others...

just rumors, but not good ones. For the past month, she's come in most mornings hungover and worse for wear, but there's more to it. I can see it, I just can't put my finger on it. Unfortunately, that's all I know. But it's enough that we need to do something."

"So, do something."

"Colleen!"

Something in her brother's voice pierced through a layer of compartments. Even buried deep, she understood very few things in life brought Augustus to this level of pique. He had always been content to keep to himself, and never more so than the past eighteen months. The last time he'd let himself worry so much over a sister, things had not ended so well. That he was here now... it was important. More important than running away.

"Okay," she said, exhaling. She closed her eyes. "Okay."

"You'll talk to her then?"

No, not that. "I'll handle it. Go back to your little office, and your little business, and your own little world."

"That's not fair," he said. "I'm here, aren't I?"

"Nothing's fair," Colleen said.

SHE WOULD REGRET THIS. OF THAT, SHE HAD ABSOLUTELY no doubt. Colleen could feign ignorance, but it would be a weak defense, for she knew Charles possessed not a reasonable bone in his body.

But she couldn't have this conversation with Evangeline without having the other, and one was impossible. Charles would solve this, even if his solution would involve a level of permanence she might later find it hard to live with.

Colleen found him in the parlor, which he'd turned into his makeshift office. An office for what, she didn't know. Charles had never known or desired work, but it didn't stop him from sitting at the desk, cigarette dangling precariously, pen bobbing while his thoughts went wherever they went.

Through Rory, she'd known a little of what her oldest brother had been up to this spring, but, like many things, she'd found a safe compartment for this information. Seeing him now, disheveled with his shirt half-open and his face soaked in sweat brought trickles to the surface.

"What do you want?" he barked.

"You look terrible." Her thoughts became words before she could stop them. Just one of the side effects of being someone else.

"Yeah? You're no Cheryl Tiegs."

"I need your help."

Charles took a hard drag from his cigarette and stubbed it out in the mountainous pile of butts pouring out of the ashtray. "Trouble staying up to study? We have a few options. Mollies will keep you up all night, but one hell of a headache in the morning. I can score some powder, but that shit's addicting if you don't know what you're doing, and it's safe to say your shape is square. LSD is always an alternative, but everyone responds differently. It might actually *put* you to sleep, which is what you're trying to avoid. Quads are also out."

Colleen grimaced. "Not that kind of help."

"No?" He reached for the pack of Marlboros, found it empty, and chucked it across the room. "Afraid I'm not good for much else."

"There's at least one other thing you're good at," Colleen said, hedging. Even committed to the idea of soliciting his help, she knew what a terrible decision it was.

Charles spread his legs and leaned his elbows onto his knees. "I'm intrigued. This better be good."

She told him all Augustus had shared. The words came easily—too easily—and she was angry at herself, for not being stronger, or strong enough to avoid this.

But there wasn't anyone else. Maureen and Elizabeth would be no help with this, and Irish Colleen was out of the question.

"I'll get my spies on it tonight," Charles said, a new excitement taking over his haggard appearance. His face brightened, and there was a glow about him, like new life, or air entering an old, shriveled balloon for the first time in years. "Tuesdays and Fridays this space club meets?"

"Astronomy," she said, and the dread swelled within her. "And yes. But she meets with these kids almost every night, according to Augustus."

He scribbled notes on the back of an envelope. "I think I know the fucker who leads this bullshit."

"You do?"

"Ethan Summerland. Trust-fund dipshit, deals to all the Uptown kids. Never runs out of supply, and he doesn't discriminate on age."

"You know this, because..."

"Because he's *my* fucking dealer, Colleen. Or one of them. I detest the piece of shit, but he's the only one in town who can get Colombian cocaine, and so until some of these other fuckers step up their game—"

Colleen held up her hands. "I get it."

"Any-fucking-way, he uses his parents' *pied-a-terre* on Dauphine for his business, which is more than slinging dope. A lot more. I don't care *how* fucking boss his coke is, he does not get to fuck with my sister."

"Information only, Charles," Colleen said, and now the dread was full-blown, an organ all its own, come to life. Her words were hollow and meaningless, for why else would she have told him if not for him to take care of the problem so she could forget it and return to her land of oblivion?

"Yeah." Charles didn't turn, didn't look at her as he tapped the pen on the desk. "Yeah, information only."

CHARLES DIDN'T NEED HIS SPIES. HE DIDN'T TELL Colleen this, because she didn't need to be nosy about *everything*. He already knew about Ethan's parties. What went on. The nature of the clientele.

What he couldn't wrap his mind around was what Evangeline

had to do with any of it. That strange little genius stomping around the house in camo and combat boots and hair like a million tiny corkscrews didn't belong anywhere near that crowd. They'd chew her up and spit her out without missing a beat, and she'd never even know what hit her or why.

He happened to know Ethan reserved Wednesdays for cutting the blow and counting scratch. No parties. No sales. That would be a perfect time to pay him a visit. To have a "chat," man to man.

In the meantime, he had another family matter to sort out.

Charles revved the engine of the Trans Am and peeled out into the afternoon sun.

THE CEMENT WAS COLD BENEATH HIM, EVEN AFTER THE hours he'd sat upon it. He couldn't make himself lie down on the slab, no matter how hard his eyes fought to stay open. He knew the kind of men who'd been here before him.

What he still couldn't figure out was *why* the cops had been waiting for him at Elizabeth's school. How did they know? It's not like he'd told anyone. He hadn't even told Elizabeth, unless...

Jesus. Had she seen it? Had she known and tried to stop him, her own brother? Had him set up to rot in jail?

Augustus showed up around midnight. He could have come sooner, but making him wait, making him sweat it out, was a message, clearly.

Well, message fucking received.

He didn't see Augustus stepping up to do right by Elizabeth. Or Colleen, or Evangeline, or Maureen. If not him, then who? Certainly not their mother, who preferred to extend her help only so far as her judgment.

The officer handed the bag with Charles' wallet, keys, watch, and smokes to Augustus, as if Charles wasn't there and hadn't just signed for it.

"Thanks, dick," he muttered with a snort, and the officer pretended not to hear it.

"You can get your car from the impound when it opens Monday," the officer shot back.

Augustus said nothing on the walk to the car, and still nothing for the first mile or so on the road. At the corner of St. Charles and Third, he turned in and parked the car along the curb, then switched it off.

"We gonna walk from here?"

Augustus leaned back in the driver's seat and closed his eyes.

"You've really done it this time, Huck. You know that, right?"

Charles snickered. "That? They dropped the charges. I didn't even get a chance at those kids. They've got intent, nothing else."

"If only it was just that. Look." Augustus shifted in his seat, to face him. Dark circles rimmed the lower half of his eyes, as if he hadn't already looked sufficiently put-upon. "Today was a big day for the family. A bad day."

"Rub it in."

"You getting arrested was just the tip of the iceberg, I'm afraid."

"So, say it. What happened?"

Augustus ran his hand over the gearshift. "The dean called. The board reviewed your expulsion today, and the decision stands. It's permanent."

The blood drained from Charles' face and neck. "So, I'll go to Loyola. Or UNO. Who cares? Tulane isn't the only fucking college in this town, you know."

"You don't think they talk?"

"Who the fuck cares!"

"You've been in undergrad for six years. Six."

"So? Everyone works at their own pace."

"Mama also had news for us tonight at dinner. She called a family dinner, but you were... it doesn't matter. Maureen's troubles didn't end with that teacher."

"What do you mean? She fucking *another* teacher?"

"Charles, stop and just listen. No, not a teacher, at least we don't think so, but she's been promiscuous, it seems, and got herself in the family way."

Charles launched himself out of his seat so hard he hit his head. "Maureen is *pregnant*?"

"Was," Augustus said with a sigh. "Remember when we thought she was in the hospital for an appendectomy? That's not what it was. That's just what Mama told us, because she thought we couldn't handle the truth. I don't know. Mama took her to someone to perform the procedure, and things went wrong and Maureen got sick. Mama had to lie to the doctors and say Maureen tried to do it to herself with an, er, coat hanger, to avoid legal problems. They won't arrest a kid, but they'd arrest Mama. Can you imagine?"

"No," Charles said, because he couldn't imagine a damn thing with his head throbbing like this, throbbing and throbbing and throbbing. "Is that it?"

"Is that it?" Augustus shook his head. "No, actually it's not. With Maureen's and Elizabeth's troubles this year, she's pulled them both out of school. She's going to homeschool them going forward."

"Maybe that's for the best."

"But not here in New Orleans," Augustus said. He turned the key, but didn't put the car into first gear just yet. "Mama is putting Oak Haven up for sale and we're moving, to Vacherie. To Ophélie. Permanently."

SUMMER 1972

VACHERIE, LOUISIANA
NEW ORLEANS, LOUISIANA

CHAPTER 6

I See You

Charles didn't need any outward encouragement to understand his value as a man, which displayed itself most prominently as heir and protector to this vast family. He was born into this role, and none of his flaws could outshine the honor in who he was by virtue of that birth.

Yet, he never felt more enmeshed in this role than when he sat in the old oaken chair of his ancestors, in the venerable third floor office of Ophélie, reserved for the heirs alone. His father, and his before him had sat in the hard, unforgiving husk of wood, a piece of furniture that had supposedly survived the long voyage from France in the mid-nineteenth century. Somewhere along the way someone could have added a cushion of sorts to increase the comfort. But August once told his son that they should never be so comfortable they forget where they'd come from, and there was no better reminder than an aching back at the end of a long day.

The office wasn't as big as the one on the first floor, where most business was conducted over the years. Anyone in the family could, and had, used that one. It was large and inviting, with ceiling-to-floor windows, and welcoming tones of red and gold.

The heir's office was sterile and Spartan. A single desk and chair, positioned neatly in the center of the long, narrow room that stretched from front to back of the house like a lookout in an old fort, was all the room contained now, or ever. Charles used to joke about livening up the place, with posters of rock icons or fast cars, but he no longer joked about such things.

Charles hadn't known what to do with Cat when she came to see him. There was only one seat in the sparse room, and, of course, he gave it to her. He could take her to his bedroom, but the others were home, most of them anyway, and privacy would be nonexistent. Though he knew nothing would happen between them, she deserved that privacy; to be here without whispers and judgment.

Why *was* she here? He'd asked himself that as the seconds passed to minutes, as he watched her leaned back and right at home in her soft yellow sundress, gladiator sandal bobbing in the air as her leg bounced over her knee.

He could read her mind. Too bad he was so out of practice. It would require all his focus, when she deserved his full attention.

"Vacherie is a long drive," he remarked. He'd started by leaning against the desk, but the proximity belied an intimacy that bordered on presumptuous. He then gave up and used the wall, instead. "If I'd known you wanted to see me, I would have come to you."

Cat laughed. One finger traced mindless circles on her bare, but sun-kissed, lightly-freckled, knee. "How I wish I'd thought of that! You still owe me a ride in that fast car of yours, Huck."

"Name the time. The place." He hoped, fleetingly, that she might suggest they go now. At least then he could transfer his crazed heartbeat into the power of the gearshift and find his calm within his element. Here, the simplicity of the space left nothing except the two of them and his complete loss of cool.

"Some other time," Cat replied. She looked around. "Love what you've done with the place."

"It's tradition," he explained weakly. He wanted to smack himself. He had so much wittier... better... cleverer responses than that.

"Well," she said with a burgeoning smile, "we can't challenge that, can we?"

“Where’s Colin?” he asked finally, the closest he could come to the question he really wanted to ask.

Catherine uncrossed her legs and leaned forward over the desk. The gesture was startlingly less ladylike, but he liked it better. She was comfortable, though he’d done almost nothing to help her get there. “Look, I know things have been tense between the two of you since the Tulane stuff.”

The Tulane stuff. His indefinite expulsion. “I think he’s done with me.”

She smiled. “No, Huck. He loves you. We all do.”

All. “He’s right to be done.” Charles let the honesty flow out. He’d never had any desire to let anyone past the front door of his thoughts and feelings, but Cat did more than put him at ease. She soothed him. “I’d be done with me, too.”

“Stop feeling sorry for yourself,” she said. The sharpness in her voice caused his head to whip up so fast a wave of nausea passed over. “The Charles I know would pick himself up off the floor of this very special office and find a way.”

Charles sputtered through a failed reply. He finally stopped trying. His jaw hung half-open, helpless.

“You’ll catch flies,” she teased, and he recovered himself.

“College wasn’t for me, anyway,” Charles said. He’d told himself this with every failed grade, every call from the dean. A way of rationalizing something and making it inevitable. But there was truth to the statement all along. He’d never use a degree for anything beyond wall decoration.

“It isn’t for everyone,” she agreed. “What will you do, then?”

“I’m not sure.” He flexed his hands, then shoved them in his pocket, driving them deep, an anchor of sorts to steady him. To keep his “other” mind from taking off in an embarrassing direction. He wondered if any woman had ever before sat in the heir’s chair as she did now. Then he stopped himself, as the thought of taking her in that chair, the soft thumps of the uneven legs keeping rhythm, produced a deeply inopportune throb.

“Have you thought about traveling?”

"Traveling?"

Cat swept her dainty arms across the room, likely imagining the whole world coming to life before her. "The world! Have you been outside New Orleans much?"

He hadn't, not since his father died, which was a damn shame considering there was nothing to hold them back. But Irish Colleen had held tight to those things, those basic human needs that kept the world turning. She had no room in her life for wanderlust, or other whims. "Not really. But... I will. When I have a family."

She nodded slowly. "For most, having a family makes it harder to travel. You'll never have to worry about such things, I suppose."

Charles had never been ashamed of his money, but the comment gave him pause. He wanted to insist he had other worries, ones she couldn't even begin to understand, but that would make things so much worse. If she knew the things he'd done, she wouldn't be sitting in his chair for long.

This brief reminder of who he was helped him become that man again. Brash, bold, unafraid to speak his mind. "Cat, why are you here? Without Colin, I mean."

Cat's golden hair fell over her shoulders as she stood and crossed the room, coming toward him. "It's not the 1800s, Huck. I don't need a chaperon to visit a man."

"You *know* what I mean." She was within reach now, and his hand traveled through the air and landed at the surface of her silken hair. He hesitated only a half second before he let her hair run through his fingers. He guided it behind her shoulders and out of the way.

Her eyes followed the gesture with a curious grin. "I know how it is to be lonely."

Charles smirked. "I'm never lonely."

"No, you're never alone," she said. "And there's a difference."

"What are you saying?"

"I'm saying, I know Colin is your rock. He's mine, too. I get it. I do. But you must know he's never going to cheer you on when you make mistakes, and sometimes, he'll run and hide, like he's doing now, to teach you a lesson."

"Is that what he's doing? Teaching me a lesson?"

She shrugged. He couldn't stop staring at her collarbone, which was just the slightest shade of peach from the summer sun. "Maybe that's what he thinks he's doing. Why did I come? I don't know. I asked myself that on the whole drive over." She laughed. "I can't speak for Colin, and I won't try. He'll come around, but in the meantime, you need to know you're not a bad man, Charles."

His mouth was so dry that when he swallowed he nearly choked. "You don't know me, Cat."

She pressed her hands, fingers splayed to his chest. On one finger, he saw the little ruby Colin had given her for their one-year. "I do know you, Huck. I know you're a good man. I see you. I see through to the real you."

"The real me." The words felt imperceptible, no more than a whisper.

"Sounds like a bunch of bologna, I know, but I've always been a good judge of character."

"And how are you so sure I'm that man?"

Her fingers moved ever so slightly against his chest and a gasp traveled up from the spot, caught in the back of his throat. "I just am. And I'm never wrong."

"You came all the way out here to tell me that?"

"I did."

"Because you *see* me."

"I see you."

"And?"

Cat's hand fell away. "And I suspect no one ever has before. I thought to myself, my friend is hurting and maybe I can help him. I know what it's like to be the outcast."

"You?" He stopped his laugh before it was fully formed. She was serious.

"Everyone in my family has become something great. Doctors. Lawyers. That was never the life for me. I've always wanted to be a poet, and while I'll get that business degree, I'll never be anything but a poet. You'd think I murdered the president or something, though. My family can't see past that failure to see that I'm happy."

Charles didn't think happy women showed up alone to see overly available men, but he kept this to himself. "That's the stupidest thing I've ever heard," he said, and when he saw her face, quickly added, "Your parents. Who cares if you want to write poetry? We have enough fucking doctors and lawyers. And you can tell Colin I said so."

Cat laughed at this. "I will. I'm meeting him in an hour, and I'll tell him you said so."

Charles reached forward and grabbed her hand. "I wouldn't. Tell him you talked to me, I mean."

She withdrew her hand. "Yeah, you're probably right."

CHARLES WATCHED HER AS SHE DESCENDED THE WIDE porch and then navigated through the gravel, toward her small car. He waved and waited until her car was turned around and headed the almost half-mile down the driveway and back toward River Road.

"What was Catherine Connelly doing here?" Colleen asked, appearing behind him. "And alone?"

"Beats the shit out of me."

"She was here quite a while."

Charles spun and glared at her. "And what the fuck do you know about it?"

"I'm the one who answered the door."

"Oh." Charles scratched the back of his head. "Yeah, hey, Colleen," he called to her as she walked away. "About the Evangeline stuff..."

She brightened. "You have info now?"

Charles shook his head. "I just wanted you to know I handled it."

Colleen stepped closer again, eyes narrowing. "What does that mean, you handled it?"

"It *means*, you can say thank you, Charles, and not fucking concern yourself about it anymore."

"Charles..." Her tone was warning.

"Hey," he said, "we both know you wouldn't have come to me, of all people, if you just wanted to talk to these assholes. Right? Right." He patted her head. "So, it's done. You can stop worrying, wipe that pretend shocked look off your face, and that's that."

CHAPTER 7
Sleeping Dogs and All That

Maureen didn't think things could get any worse, but that was before she began waking at night to the cries of a baby. Deep, soul-cutting screams, not of anything so simple as hunger or discomfort, but of sheer agony. The despair of what would never be.

It didn't matter anymore, what was real and what was her imagination. What was the difference, when she had no control over either? Whether she was actually hearing the cries of her perpetually unborn child each night, or her imagination was finding unique methods of punishment, the result was the same.

She wasn't sleeping at all anymore, not that she'd ever slept well in this decrepit relic so far from the rest of the living. At least their old mansion in the Garden District was ensconced in the outside world, only a streetcar ride away from where things really happened. Here, they were a half-mile from even a road, and on that road were miles and miles of sugarcane and nothingness. The river raged on the other side, relentless and forbidding.

Being bedridden for weeks hadn't helped matters. The man Maureen's mother had sought out to "fix the problem" had finished the job, but left her bleeding and in physical torment, to the point her mother commented she might never have children if she didn't heal soon. Irish Colleen wouldn't allow her oldest daughters to use their healing powers on her, and if there was ever a sign her mother didn't love her, this was it. Colleen and Evangeline could have taken away every last drop of her pain, and they were begging for the chance to do so. But Irish Colleen held her ground, for reasons she didn't feel it prudent to share with anyone, and instead tended to Maureen's bedside herself, as if she had any idea how to heal her through the horrors she'd been through.

"Don't forget I was a nursemaid," she pointed out as she wrung the bloody cloth in the basin.

"For a dying woman!" Maureen returned, and Irish Colleen had no argument, because it was true. Her only experience as a nursemaid was in tending to her future husband's dying wife. And what skill was required to administer regular doses of Morphine, or dabbing at the poor woman's cracked and drying skin with a damp cloth?

Colleen snuck in one day while she was sleeping. Maureen awoke to her sister's hands hovering over her, and tears glistening in her eyes.

"What are you doing?" Maureen asked, though she knew.

"You shouldn't have to suffer like this. Not when there's another way."

"We suffer because we were born."

"Maybe," Colleen said. "But I'll be damned if these gifts were for nothing but pain."

"Colleen! Don't you *dare* go against my wishes!"

Irish Colleen's small but booming presence in the door—Maureen, over the years, had wondered if her mother didn't have a hint of magic in her, after all, for she always seemed to know precisely when someone was about to disobey her—was the line of separation between Maureen's complete suffering, and even a small reprieve.

Small, because Colleen couldn't fix the problem that would ail her long after her womb healed.

"You need to leave," Madeline said, looking more forlorn than usual. "Find a way, Maureen. Any way you can. It will always be like this if you don't. Mama can't help herself."

"Please, don't listen to your sister," their father warned. "She'd be with you, instead of me, if she had only found her patience. Your mother loves you, and she's doing her best."

"You don't know, Daddy. You don't know what it was like," Madeline said and then disappeared in a fit of stubborn anger.

"Why, Maureen?" asked Peter, against the anguished wailing of an infant that was not gone and not forgotten.

MAUREEN KNEW OF NO ONE IN THEIR FAMILY WHO possessed an ability that could help her find a way to take away her own. She wouldn't even know what to call that, or where to start. She suspected that it wasn't an ability that could help her, anyway. What she needed was something deeper, more powerful. A bigger magic.

For years, she'd heard the rumors that Pansy and her mother, Winnifred—who had married into the Guidry family when she settled down with Pierce, and was rather unspectacular in her own right—had been dabbling in black magic. Winnifred Babin's family were trappers from New Iberia, whose home purportedly ran up against the shack of Adelphe Baptiste, the most well-known and feared voodoo priestess in Iberia Parish. Adelphe's husband, Anton, was a trapper, too, and would go out for runs with Winnifred's father. One day, Anton's foot slipped when balancing on a log, and he went careening into a dense corner of the swamp. Winnifred's father was quick to respond and saved his life, for he'd landed in a bull's den during mating season. Many of the trappers of New Iberia had stories to tell, and limbs and digits lost to the gators to go with them. But Adelphe had never forgotten what the Babin family had done for her, and the women grew closer after the incident.

Maureen loved gossip, of course, even if it did sound ridiculous. It was fun to whisper about and even spread yourself, especially when you'd come into something extra juicy, but everyone knew there was less truth than fluff in a good story. But even Colleen had talked about Pansy and Winnie's late nights in Bayou St. John, and Colleen detested people who told tales.

Pansy stopped going for a bit when she married Placide, but she's back at it now, and Pierce is beside himself. But he'll never say a word to Winnie or his daughter. He doesn't have it in him to say no.

Voodoo, Rory had whispered, because, of course Colleen hadn't said these words *to* Maureen. She'd overheard her sister telling Rory about it. Pillow talk, probably, a concept she knew about only from the whispers of her friends, because she'd never experienced it herself.

Don't listen to rumors, Rory. Voodoo is a peaceful practice with very deep roots, but there are bad apples in every religion. Even ours.

Maureen was banking on the bad apples for what she needed.

Pansy was more than happy to meet with her. Her cousin suggested coffee at Morning Call, down at the French Market, but Maureen was impatient and didn't want to waste any time. What they would hopefully do together was best done in private. Where no one could see her lose her mind when her ghosts belayed her. Instead, she asked to meet at their old house in the Garden District, which was on the market but not yet sold.

She guilt-tripped Augustus into letting her tag along with him into the city.

"How are you going to get back?" he asked. He stood before her, so much taller, almost towering over her, keys dangling at his side. She realized then how handsome her brother was. He was good-looking in an utterly unremarkable way, the kind of man who blends into a crowd until you have him alone, and can see how deep and enchanting his eyes are; how his mouth curves and his hair falls across his brow. He was better looking, even, than Charles, who all the girls did flips over and made fools of themselves for. She wondered what made one hardly noticed while the other couldn't find a moment's peace.

She realized also that she'd been alone with her brothers so few times in her life. Neither had taken much of an interest in her, and the feeling was mutual.

"I'll call someone."

Augustus' stance was defiant. "Maureen, I'm not going to be responsible for you traipsing around New Orleans by yourself. Not after…"

He didn't finish, but he could have ended with so many things, really! Not after Madeline. Not after Maureen got her teacher killed. Not after Maureen's abortion. "Well, when are you coming home?"

He shrugged and sighed. "I don't know. I might not come home tonight."

"Hot date with Carolina?"

"Carolina? You're on this, too?"

Maureen grinned. "She's so hot on you."

"Shouldn't you still be in bed resting?"

"No," Maureen said, indignant. "I'm done with that, and you would know if you were ever around."

Augustus glowered in impatience. "I have a lot to do at the office. Too much to be worrying about you."

"Then don't worry about me." An idea came to her, and it was so obvious she wondered why she hadn't thought of just telling the truth to begin with. Or, part of it. "I'm actually meeting our cousin, Pansy, if you must know. And she can take me back to Vacherie."

"Pansy? Guidry?" Augustus frowned. His mouth curled in thought, and she knew he was struggling between fighting her and believing her. "Does Mama know?"

"Mama is out making groceries."

"Fine. But you're going to leave her a note."

Maureen blanched. Mama had never had the highest opinion of the Guidrys, who she called the "colorful trash" of the family. But Pansy was still her cousin, and she had a right to see her people, regardless of what her mother thought of them. She didn't have to know *why* she was seeing Pansy. "Okay," she said and scribbled her note on the pad on the old antique dresser by the door. "Ready?"

Augustus had the look of a man who was already deeply regretting his decision. He stalked out the door and she followed.

PANSY WAS SITTING ON THE FRONT STEPS OF OAK HAVEN when Augustus dropped Maureen off. He waved at Pansy, gave Maureen an intentional look that didn't require words, and pulled away.

"Hey," Maureen said, feeling abruptly awkward in the face of realizing she hardly knew Pansy, who was closer in age to Charles. Pansy, who looked ten years older with her high-coiffed Dolly Parton curls, her neck hidden deep in the collar of her frilly dress.

"Why, Maureen, aren't you just a dream!" Pansy exclaimed and bounced down the stairs, arms wide. She pulled her into a hug as if they'd been waiting for this moment years now. "Tell me, how's your mama and 'em?"

"Good," Maureen said, dazzled by her cousin's wide eyes and dazzling smile. Colleen had never had the highest opinion of Pansy, but Maureen couldn't help but be drawn in by what felt like authentic joy to see her.

"Good, good," Pansy replied and looped her arm around Maureen's waist. Her long, fake nails scratched through the fabric. "You've got a key, I assume?"

Maureen cursed. "I knew I forgot something."

"You think I ain't never picked a lock before?" Pansy said with a wink. She fished a thin piece of metal from her bra.

Maureen gaped at her. "Do you always carry that with you?"

"You need to ask yourself why you *don't*, my dear," Pansy replied and went to work on the front door. Maureen whipped her head around, sure they'd be caught and hauled off to jail. Boy, would Augustus be mad, then.

A minute later, they were in. Maureen's heart raced as the moment drew near, when she would finally tell her secret to someone still in the land of the living. She didn't know if she could do it... if she had the courage. And what was courage, anyway? Maybe it was a fancy way of saying you're better off stupid.

Pansy's hand landed on her forearm. "Darlin', I know you didn't bring me here to catch up on old times. We hardly know one another."

"I... it's just..."

"Spit it out, girl. Does no good to hold onto poison."

"I've never told anyone, and I'm not sure I should."

"You wouldn't be here if that were true," Pansy said. She slipped the metal shimmy back in her dress. "Whatever it is, you can trust me. I've got no reason to share your secrets, and I've enough of my own."

Maureen fell back against the couch and recoiled a bit when she realized it was covered in a furniture shroud. Dead and gone, like her happiness. "My mother can't know. My brothers... my sisters..."

"They can go on minding their own business."

Should she trust Pansy? There seemed no deception in her... she was a strange bird, like all Guidrys, but Maureen didn't detect anything that worried her, beyond her own nerves and fears. This was a woman who snuck off into the swamp to practice voodoo with her mother, and somehow kept this from her husband. She knew darkness and secrets.

"My ability is ruining my life," she said finally.

Pansy grinned from the corner of her mouth. "Not the first one in this family to say so."

"I might be the only one in this family who's truly cursed, though."

"We're all cursed, thanks to Brigitte." Pansy crossed herself, kissed her fingers, and looked north to Jesus. "But go on, tell me."

"I can see and talk to the dead," Maureen blurted out. "How's that for cursed?"

Pansy leaned forward slowly. "Ya don't say?"

"I do say," Maureen snipped. "Not all of them, but the ones that matter. My father. Madeline." She paused. She couldn't mention Peter. That was a secret too far. "My dead baby."

Pansy clutched at her chest. "Maureen, say that again?"

"You heard me right. My dead baby. Mama forced me to get an abortion against my will."

Pansy's fingers were a flurry again at her chest, and she paused longer to complete a prayer. "My God, Maureen. You poor dear. You've been dealing with this all alone, haven't you?"

The tears came without warning. Maureen nodded. "I can't live like this anymore. I can't do it. It's constant, all the time, and I can't escape it."

Pansy's hand traveled to her belly. "Placide and I will be parents in the new year. I can't imagine what you must be feeling. The Lord has finally seen fit to bring our Rex into the world." Her hand fell away. "You came to me because you think I can help."

"I... well... I've heard you and your mama..."

Pansy laughed. "Do you always believe what you hear, Maureen?"

Maureen sputtered again and Pansy reached forward to steady her. "I'm just pickin'. 'Course I can help. But first I gotta ask you something, and I need you to be perfectly honest with me, and mostly, yourself."

Maureen sniffed and wiped the back of her hand across her nose. "Okay."

"I see perfectly why you think this is a curse," Pansy said, nodding to herself, "I do. But many would also see it as a gift."

"Not me!"

"Not you," Pansy agreed. "But if we can fix this, and I think we can, you'll never see your daddy again. You'll never see your sister again. You might think you're okay with this now, but final is final. Sleeping dogs and all that."

"The rest of my family will never see them again, so why should I be any different? That's how death works."

Pansy continued nodding. "If my daddy died, I'd do anything in the world to keep him around. But I s'pose I can say that because he ain't dead and he ain't haunting me. But I still gotta ask once more. Are you sure this is what you want?"

"I've never been more sure of anything in my life!" Maureen cried through her tears. "And you have no idea what it's like. You think you'd miss him, but it's not the same, not at all. It's not even close. It's horrible."

Pansy looked away, thinking. "All right, then," she said. "I brought some things along in the trunk, just in case, so I'll go get 'em and we'll get this exorcism moving right along, and have both of us home in time for dinner. Sound like a plan?"

AUGUSTUS HAD BEEN SNEEZING ALL DAY. THE insulation was finally being installed after months of him tripping over it, or regarding it with open hostility as he walked around it. Twice he'd considered why the insulation was troubling him so. He should have adapted to the foreign intrusion far sooner, and he realized the absence of this evolution was intentional. He was *intentionally* getting himself worked into a frenzy about something completely nonsensical.

Well, it wouldn't be an issue any longer, and he didn't know how to feel about that. Another, weirder realization had been that he almost liked the angst brought on by the piles of pink fiberglass half-blocking his hallway; enjoyed cursing its existence and mumbling frustrations at the audacity. None of this was like him, and maybe that was the appeal. He didn't know what to make of that, and so he didn't make anything of it.

The printing press had been installed earlier in the week, and he and Evangeline gawked over it like a couple of excited children, despite his outward protests that it wasn't a toy. But even he had run his hands across the plastic and steel, mouth agape in wonder. Somehow it was this—not the building, the desks, the construction—that made his dream come to life the most vividly. It was real now. He had the tangible instrument with which to reach his goals.

Fall, he'd told Evangeline. Fall was when they would release their first issue of Deschanel Magazine, even though he could have done it sooner. He had hundreds of submissions from worthy journalists, and not because anyone had high expectations of his publication but because of who he was. He could have put out the call for submissions for a magazine covering the lives of cross-dressing cats and the interest would have been there.

He didn't like that. He'd always wanted to make his own name in the world. But there was nothing to be done about it. There was no changing the name he was born with, and everything that came along with it. That was why he'd just gone on and named the damn magazine after himself. Why not? He'd have to prove he was worthy beyond his name, and that would take time.

Augustus heard the loud clomp-clomp of her boots long before Evangeline arrived, winded and panting. She doubled over her knees with dramatic gasps.

"Any particular reason you're using the office as a track?" Augustus asked.

Evangeline held up one finger without lifting her head. He couldn't see her face at all. It was hidden behind the storm of curls and frizz.

"Anything can be a track if you're so inclined," Evangeline replied between gulps for air. She uncoiled herself and blew out a deep breath. "I just got back from reception. Mama called."

Augustus tensed. "Everything okay at home?"

"Yeah, why wouldn't it be?"

"For one, you're..." He stopped. Evangeline, for all her genius, often missed the nuance of behavior. But then, so did he. "What did she want?"

"I don't know. Something about moving some furniture around?"

"Seriously?"

Evangeline shrugged. "She can't find Charles, but what else is new?"

"This can't wait?"

"Why are you asking me?"

Augustus sighed. "Did she say anything else?"

"I don't think so." Evangeline wiped a bead of sweat from her furrowed brow. "So, you're going?"

"Doesn't look like I have a choice."

"One always has a choice."

"Why do I always get the feeling you'd be perfectly happy as a Chinese philosopher?"

Evangeline frowned deeper. "I don't like philosophy."

Augustus swiped his keys from the top of the nearby desk. His eyes caught that strange sign Carolina had brought by weeks ago. *Love is the Answer. What was the Question?* He saw it all the time; Evangeline had seen to that with her strategic placement of the thing. Once he set his office up, he wouldn't see it so much.

"You coming with?" he asked.

Evangeline waved her hand. "I'll stay in town."

"I might not be back. I don't know what Mama has up her sleeve."

"It's fine," she said. "I'm good. Promise."

AUGUSTUS SPENT THE AFTERNOON RESHUFFLING THE attic. There was no strategy involved in the task that he could see, nor any real benefit to the restructure. Their attic at Ophélie had been cluttered for years, and even with rearranging the mess, it was still a mess. But Irish Colleen seemed more than thrilled with the results, without acknowledging there'd been no real objective in the task than getting Augustus home for a change.

"You're my greatest joy," she said when he was done, straining on her tiptoes to plant a kiss on his cheek. "You've never given me any trouble."

Augustus, over the years, had come to hear the unsaid words behind his mother's compliments. *No trouble, but isn't that the problem? What kind of life is it, to never have adventure?*

"Happy to help, Mama."

"Now that you're here, you'll stay for dinner? All of us are here tonight, except Charles, of course. He never is. Oh! And Carolina is here, too."

Augustus' mind traveled to the place of his best usefulness, as others exchanged pleasant conversation across the old dining table. Evangeline, who'd found some way home on her own, kept throwing meaningful looks and winks at Carolina, which he managed to gracefully dodge before the poor girl noticed. He didn't want to hurt her feelings and had no idea how she'd come to the conclusion he was worth the effort.

Colleen at one point seemed to realize Carolina's attentions were focused almost solely on her brother and had the nerve to glare at him, as if he had anything to do with it. He watched as a dawn of understanding came over her eyes. Her friendship with Carolina had all but fizzled out, until recently when Carolina had taken a renewed interest.

He wanted to defend himself, but that would mean addressing the issue he'd hoped by now would have faded away.

Irish Colleen was disappointed when he excused himself to return to town after dinner. "I'm sorry, Mama. I have night classes. And there's still a lot of work to do before fall, at the office."

"I'd hoped being home would help you see how much you're still needed here."

He kissed her. "I'll always come when I'm needed."

"But would you tell me if you needed me?"

He smiled by way of response. He had no idea what she wanted to hear, but he wouldn't lie to his mother. Not anymore. Covering for Madeline, Maureen, and Charles had done nothing but make matters worse.

Augustus dipped out the door before anyone else noticed. He'd made it all the way to the car before he heard footsteps in the gravel. He said a silent prayer it was one of his sisters, but as he looked up, before he even connected the dots, he knew.

"Hey," Carolina said. She had her hands deep in the pockets of her short shorts, so much so that the flaps from the pockets hung lower than the seams. Her long, tanned legs twisted at the ankle as she swayed back and forth.

"Hey," he replied without turning. He found he was frozen in place. The key hovered just above the door lock.

"Everyone seemed really happy to see you."

Augustus nodded. *Unlock the damn door. Get in. Say something pleasant. Leave.*

"Family is really important," she went on. He felt her grow closer, though he was still locked in suspended animation, and then heard her soft footsteps on the rocks. "It's everything."

"Yeah," he said stupidly. The growing sweat from his palm made his hands slippery, and the keys dropped from between his fingers, landing in a soft thud.

Carolina was at his feet before he could will himself to kneel down and grab them. He looked at her, and she looked up. Her smile was sad as she dropped his keys in his hand, her fingers brushing the damp flesh and lingering a moment.

She rose, and they were so close he stopped breathing. "You're hurting, Augustus, and I know what that's like."

Augustus swallowed. He closed his hands over the keys and tried to back away, but the cursed car was in the way. "I really have to go. I'll be late for class."

Carolina reached forward and wrapped her fingers through his. He was so shocked by the gesture he was completely unprepared to react to it, and he stood there, dumfounded, holding her hand. "I lost a sibling, too. A brother. To leukemia."

Some of the tension faded away. "Really? I didn't... I didn't know. I'm so sorry." He should have known, and the failure of this, of not knowing something very important about his sister's friend, burned in his cheeks. How many other things in life had he missed, nose buried in diversions?

Carolina shrugged and kicked at the gravel. A small plume of dust gathered at their feet. "I don't like to talk about it. It's the worst thing that ever happened to me, so I understand... what it's like, you know, to lose a sibling. And to not have anyone else to talk about it, you know, who understands, too."

Augustus nodded. Talking was out of the question, with anyone. Even Carolina, who might understand if he were to share the weight of his guilt. Sharing changed nothing. It didn't bring the ghosts back to the living, or cause them to end their ceaseless haunting.

"Anyway, I'll let you get to class. School is *almost* as important as family." She squeezed his fingers before dropping them, and both their hands fell away, to their sides. Her smile was brief, but full of a strange warmth that disarmed him. "I just wanted you to know I'm here for you. If you wanna talk, or if you... well, if you don't. For anything, is what I mean."

Black dots danced before Augustus' eyes as she left him there, and his breathing and heartrate started to return to normal. When he was sure she wasn't coming back, he slid into the driver's seat and closed his eyes to gather his bearings; to find himself again, and transfer whatever remained of that conversation to something useful.

CHAPTER 8

I'm Gonna Marry Him One day

Elizabeth brushed the hair on the last of the porcelain dolls. She'd already sorted the others, and they had moved back to lining the shelf above her bed. Her mother's shelf, not hers, but it was important to Irish Colleen that Elizabeth seem normal, so Elizabeth acted accordingly.

She'd never liked dolls, even as a young girl. At thirteen, she was horrified to have their small, beady eyes staring back at her from the darkness. The world, though, was a series of symbols, assigned to people and ideas, as ways of expression. Dolls were an almost universal symbol for young girls. If Elizabeth was a time traveler—there were some, supposedly, though she'd never met one—she'd go back in time and instead reverse the roles of young men and women. Give boys the dolls, she thought. Let the girls build forts and disappear into their imaginations.

When the last of her dolls was safely ensconced in the strange hell above her bed, Elizabeth went to her vanity and sat at the small, velvet seat and gave an earnest attempt at painting her face. Makeup was another thing she couldn't find interest in, but as soon as Irish Colleen mentioned she was at the age where she needed to be concerned with such things, Elizabeth, with a sigh, found her way to the drugstore and did as was expected of her.

Of course, she had not a clue how to apply it properly. In a perfect world, she could have asked her three older sisters for help, and maybe even in her imperfect world that would be okay, but she had learned years ago that the closer the contact to someone, the more she saw. The more she saw, the more she ached with the knowledge of an unchangeable future. She'd already seen far too much of Charles' future.

Her lipstick was all wrong. She smiled, then frowned, searching for the right expression to make it look all right. There wasn't one. Elizabeth ripped a tissue from the box and pulled it across her mouth with so much force she squealed out loud.

"Lizzy? Everything okay in here?"

"Yes, Mama," Elizabeth called back as she stared at her deranged face. She was a failed clown. No, a vampire. Yes, a vampire wouldn't be so bad, really. She grinned, and then immediately wiped the look away. The grin made her look more like The Joker from her Batman comics, and that was definitely not the look she was going for.

"I'll come drop your laundry by in a minute, if that's okay."

If that's okay... she announced herself for fear of what she might find in her daughter's room, and Elizabeth wondered what exactly she expected. Dead animals? Ritual sacrifice? Sure, Mom, give me a minute while I hide the carcasses. "Yeah, okay."

Elizabeth continued working at removing the strange paint, which was annoying but not unbearable. All in all, things had been better at Ophélie. School had been an untenable stress, one she couldn't do a thing about. Being in close quarters with so many children, day after day, had sent her senses into a macabre overdrive. Death, divorce, abuse, sadness. Always the darkness, never the light. Sharing was never a help to anyone but herself, a form of self-preservation akin to robbing food from your loved ones to avoid starving to death. And, oh, what if she'd shared everything? Every impending divorce, every breakup, every broken bone or fractured heart. She knew so much about her classmates she'd ceased to see them as people and instead viewed them as statistics on a rap sheet. *Ashley. Was poor, but recently moved to Second Street in a home her family could only afford because her father stole from his business partner. Mother is having an affair with the accountant. Brother will die of a rare immune disorder in San Francisco in the '80s.*

School after school, this haunted her. And how many years had she begged Irish Colleen to find another way for her to get her education? Putting a soothsayer in a public place every day of their lives was like sticking an empath in with a bunch of mental patients. She could have sped up the process, she supposed, by being honest about how many times a day she fantasized about sliding into the bath and slitting her veins from elbow to wrist, but as with most things, Elizabeth knew honesty did not always get you where you intended.

Here, in her room, she was safe. Even if she *was* afraid the dolls would one day come to life and murder her in her sleep.

There was only one thing she missed about the city, and school. One person, if she was being specific.

"I'm coming in!" Irish Colleen announced, and then waited a good five seconds before entering.

Elizabeth rolled her eyes, then turned to smile at her mother. "Thanks for washing everything."

"I could fold them, too."

Elizabeth tempered her annoyance at the eggshells her mother brought into every room she was in, every time. It only proved Irish Colleen didn't actually understand her at all. Elizabeth didn't blame herself for Madeline's death. It didn't work that way. She could see things she had no power to prevent. That's what made the whole thing so horrible. "No, Mama, I can do it."

Irish Colleen began folding the clothes anyway. "It's a nice day, outside. Not too hot for a spell. You should go play."

More things parents said because they should, not because it made sense. Elizabeth had never enjoyed the outdoors. The abundance of life only reminded her of the inevitability of death. Everything died eventually. "I'm fine in here."

"Oh, how lovely your dolls look! You're such a good Mama,"

Irish Colleen said, and Elizabeth ticked the imaginary box labeled, *Convince Mother You are Normal.*

"I said I could fold them."

"Oh, posh," Irish Colleen said, dismissing the thought. "I was thinking, Elizabeth."

Not again. "Oh?"

"Huck, Augustus, Colleen, and Evie have their lives and friends outside of Ophélie." She stacked the folded clothing in neat piles as she worked. "I didn't consider what it might be like for you and Maureen." She paused, holding a shirt in the air, thinking. "Not Maureen so much, her friends are... anyhow, if there's anyone you'd like to invite out here, to play, we can arrange for that."

"Connor," Elizabeth blurted out before her mother's words had even cooled.

"Connor?" Irish Colleen stopped again. "Do I know him?"

"Sullivan."

"Sullivan... as in *the* Sullivans?"

"Yes, *the* Sullivans. Connor is a cousin of Colin and Rory."

"I see." She returned to the laundry, but with less fervor. "And Connor is your friend?"

Irish Colleen said the words so casually, as if friends came easily for Elizabeth. As if they ever stayed long.

"He's my best friend." Elizabeth swallowed her pride. "My only friend."

"Well, I suppose we could invite him out every now and then to spend time here," Irish Colleen said, in the same tone she used when dismissing any idea that she didn't want to argue about.

"I'm going to marry him someday," Elizabeth said, completely unsure as to why she said it. And to her mother, of all people, who regarded whimsy the way others regarded a mosquito landing on their arm.

Irish Colleen's head fell to the side. She chuckled. "Is that right?"

"Yes, that's right," Elizabeth said. Her cheeks were on fire. She regretted the words, but there was no going back now.

"That's sweet, but don't you think our family is already wrapped up enough with the Sullivans? Charles and Colin are best friends, though it makes no sense to anyone. Colleen and Rory—"

"Aren't together anymore."

"For now. Maureen and Chelsea can't decide if they're friends or enemies, and the answer apparently depends on the alignment of the planets or something, to hear your sister tell it. And, she doesn't want me to know this, but I *do* know Evangeline dated Patrick for a spell last year, and before that, he dated Mad..." The thought trailed off. "What's next? Augustus and Chelsea?"

"Chelsea is sixteen, Mama. She's five years younger than Aggie."

"And I was barely eighteen when I had Charles. Your father was forty-five."

There was no such thing as an argument that Irish Colleen didn't win, so Elizabeth didn't waste her breath explaining how her comparisons were meaningless in context. Logical fallacies were a particular specialty of Colleen Brady. "What do you have against the Sullivans anyway?"

"Nothing," her mother replied in haste. "They've been very good to our family."

What a strange response that was. Very good to our family. "You asked me about friends, Mama. Connor is my friend. I don't care what his last name is, and neither should you. He isn't afraid of me like the other kids were."

Irish Colleen turned to her. "He knows about you?"

Elizabeth nodded. "The Sullivans have their parlor tricks, too, you know."

"What on earth are you talking about?"

"Some of them can do stuff, like we can. Slide things across tables. Reads minds."

Irish Colleen returned to her folding. "That's ridiculous, Elizabeth. If the Sullivans were like you kids, we would've known about it. I can't believe you told him."

Elizabeth shrugged. "I've told other kids, too, Mama, he's just the only one who believed me."

"They've been around us so long, it's no wonder they've learned a few things about your father's side. I just hope they know to mind their business."

"They're our attorneys. They know about discretion."

"Connor isn't bound by such rules. He's a kid," Irish Colleen said, but her shoulders had begun to sag and Elizabeth could see she was tired of arguing.

"If you want me to have friends, you can't be so picky," Elizabeth said.

"Fine." The word came out more as a sigh. "You're right. Feel free to call him and invite him over, as long as his mother is fine with it."

She would be. She hardly paid attention to anything her children did. "Okay, I will. Thanks, Mama."

Irish Colleen put the folded laundry into the appropriate dresser drawers and then slid the laundry basket under her arm. "But please stop talking about who you're going to marry. When you say things like that, I never know whether you're being a silly girl or if you've seen something."

Elizabeth grinned and turned away.

CHAPTER 9

Everyone Just Dies

Charles' day had been utterly unremarkable, at least in the way all his days were. He'd awoken in the bed of a woman whose name escaped him, with a hangover that could win awards. He'd stumbled home to Ophélie around noon, narrowly avoiding wrecking his precious Trans Am on that unforgiving bend in River Road, right past the turnoff from LA-20, and then slept the night off, waking when the sun began to crest over the western side of the property, reflecting off the water of the Mississippi just over the levee.

His evening was an entirely different matter.

Charles had been thinking of a way to avoid dinner with the family. Irish Colleen was certain to ride his ass for something. It didn't matter what, she'd either bring something up from a decade ago or start in on something he had nothing to do with, like the war, and he was damn tired of answering to her when this was *his* house. She may be his mother, but her most important job, the one August had left her with that stood above all others, was to see his oldest son become the heir of the family. Well, Charles was the heir now, a man grown several years, and he shouldn't have to skulk around his own house, hiding from his mother, from the shame she tried to heap upon his shoulders.

Several phones rang throughout the house in unison. Ophélie was so big that there were phones all over the old plantation, so there was never an excuse for a call to go unanswered. Unless it was up to him, of course. That's what they had Richard and Condoleezza for, not to mention their cache of staff who were always getting in the way.

The ringing stopped. Charles pulled a pillow from the cold side of his bed and pressed the soft fabric to his face. He was always so hot when he woke up. Evangeline once told him it was because sleep was when the body healed, and he'd done so much damage it had to work extra hard. He wondered if half the shit she said was true. If he hadn't spent six years in college, and still failed out, he might know the answer.

"Charles!" Colleen's voice bounced across the oak and cypress, carrying down the hall.

He set the pillow aside and groaned. "What?"

"Phone for you!"

"If it's another reporter—" he screamed just as Colleen was saying, "it's Catherine!"

Charles shot up in bed. Cat? He'd seen her twice since her strange visit to Ophélie, both times double dates with Colin. But she'd never said a word about their conversation, and after a while, he'd begun to think he might have hallucinated the whole thing. That made a hell of a lot more sense than Cat driving an hour from New Orleans to espouse his merits as a man.

Colleen thrust his door open. "Hey, did you hear me?"

Charles nodded, only half-aware of her standing there. He looked around... for what? His head screamed. These cursed headaches were worse in the summer, and especially in the bedrooms, which rarely cooled down all the way in the old house.

"Don't you have a phone in here?"

Yes, that was it! "Yeah... somewhere..."

Colleen huffed and stormed across the room, to his dresser. She pulled out drawer after drawer until she found it. She held the yellow metal over her head like a prize, the long cord dangling.

"Be a doll and plug it in?"

She rolled her eyes, but did as he asked. She held the receiver to her ear and waited, then said, "Cat, you still there? Yeah, I found him. Hang on." She held it out.

Charles nodded to the door.

"Sure, yeah, you're welcome." Colleen went to leave, then turned when she reached the door again. "Don't tie up the line too long. Elizabeth is waiting for a call."

Charles shooed her away. "Cat? You there?"

"I'm here." He could hardly hear her, but there was something in her voice that immediately sent off the alarms in him.

"One second." He waited until he heard the other receiver click. "Cat? What's wrong?"

"I just broke up with Olly." She sobbed on the other end. "He just left."

"What?" Charles looked around the room, as if it would provide some guidance on what to say other than just single syllable words. "Why?"

"I... tried to talk to him, but he is so hard-headed! When he has his mind set on something being true, you can't change it." She blew her nose into something and returned to sobbing.

Charles knew this was an important moment. She'd broken up with Colin and it wasn't one of her girlfriends she'd called, but him. And she'd said she'd been the one to do it. He started to ask why she was crying if it was her idea to break up, but something inside him cautioned what a bad idea that would be. "Okay, okay. It's okay." *You can do better than that, you ape.* "I'm sorry. Do you wanna talk about it?"

"You know him!" she cried, as if that explained everything. "You know how he can be. How he gets."

"Yeah, Colin is pretty fucking stubborn," Charles agreed. "But you've been with him a long time, and you knew that. Something must have happened?"

"Oh, it happened all right! I tried to just tell him how I was feeling, but we both know he doesn't relate to *feelings*, not when there's logic on the line."

"Cat," Charles said softly. "Start at the beginning."

"Okay," she said, sniffling. "You know how he's starting his law internship in the fall?"

"Yeah."

"I already don't see him as much as I want to, and he was reading off his schedule and all the things he'll be doing, and I realized it wasn't going to leave much time for us." She stopped for a moment and he heard her take a drink of something. "That should matter, too, right? Time for us?"

"Yeah, of course it should." Charles ransacked the drawer for anything to take the edge off the headache. He had to think clearly. This was important... why, he wasn't sure yet, but it was, and he had to be present. He found some pills, painkillers he'd stolen from his mother when she got her gall bladder out, and popped two.

"He sure didn't seem to think so. He asked me why that was so important, and I told him, we'll be hitting two years this winter, and I don't want to spend less time, I want to spend more. He asked me what I thought the whole point of going to law school was, that he was preparing for our future together, and I probably *shouldn't* have said this, but I said... well, I said he wasn't doing that for me, it was for his Sullivan ego."

"Damn," Charles said with an exhale. Even he knew you didn't attack a Sullivan for their pride.

"But then I tried to calm down and try another approach. I told him... I said, if you really feel all these activities and classes are unavoidable, then why don't we move in together? We spend all our time at either his place or mine anyway. It's more practical, if nothing else! But it would help us with the time issue, because we'd have mornings and nights, and..." She dissolved into her grief again, and for several moments he listened to her keen and cough.

"Look, Cat... Colin is a complicated—"

"So then he asked me if I didn't think maybe I was rushing things! Rushing things? Charles, I've been with him almost *two years.* He was the first one of us to mention marriage, and he talks as if that's still what he wants. But *I'm* rushing things?"

Colin had much to teach Charles about the world, had he the desire to learn, but this was an area Charles wished his friend would take occasional advice from him on. He had no doubt of Colin's love for Catherine... he'd never seen him so serious about anything, or anyone, not ever. But Colin's approach to the world would always be one of logic first, and to him, everything made sense when he could categorize it into neat little boxes.

But a defense of Colin wasn't why Cat had called him. "Shit, Cat, I'm so sorry."

"So I told him we were done. I'm not going to throw any more of my life away waiting for someone who might never appreciate me."

"I'm sure he'll realize what an ass he's been and come crawling back in the morning."

"No," she said, blowing her nose again. "Nope. I don't care if he does. I'll tell him to go waste some other girl's time."

Charles wasn't much of an authority on serious relationships, but he'd comforted enough heartbroken women to know that even the most serious words said in anger and hurt rarely meant much the next day. "Are you at home? Is your roommate there?"

There was silence on her end, and then she said, very seriously, "Why? Do you want to come over?"

His heartbeat dropped to the organ between his legs. Oh, God, did he ever want to come over. And for the first time in his life, he wasn't looking to fuck, he wanted to try something else entirely, *making love*, whatever that was, he wanted to figure it out with Cat. To look into her eyes as he drove inside her, to see them roll back in her head as she cried out from her first orgasm.

"Charles? You still there?"

"Yeah." He ran his tongue over his lips, which had gone dry as stone. "I'm here."

"Jeannie isn't here. She's at her parents' in Baton Rouge for the weekend. It's just me here."

Charles had no doubt of what awaited him at Cat's apartment. He wouldn't even have to work for it... she'd fall into his arms, and into her bed, and he could have everything he'd fantasized about since the day he'd first seen her smile at him. He could have *all* of it, and maybe she'd even date him for a while after, until she realized the rottenness seeping out from his core.

But he loved Colin, the way he loved Augustus. Colin was his brother, through and through, no matter what. And though Colin hadn't handled his breakup with Cat well, Colin loved her with all his heart. If Charles stayed away, they'd be back together in the morning; maybe even that night. But not if he went to see her.

"I... Cat, I'd love to come see you." He squinted and pounded his fist against his thigh, breathing his self-control out through his nose. "I really would."

"So, come," she whispered. "For me."

Come. He was about to do exactly that if she kept cooing invitations in his ear. "I can't," he said after another deep breath. "It's Lizzy... Mom asked me to look after her while she's in town."

"Oh, yeah. Sure. I see." She'd seen all right, directly through the lie to the truth of his deflection. He heard it in the slow withdrawal of her invitation. "It's okay. I'll call Theresa or Jamie, see if they want to see a flick or something. I think *Deliverance* just came out, and Colin would never have seen that with me in a million years."

"That sounds nice. You should do that."

"Yeah," she replied, and he knew then, he'd failed her somehow. He'd lost her, though she'd never actually been his to begin with.

"You're gonna be okay, Cat? If you really need me..." His strength faltered.

"No," she said firmly, for both of them. "I'm good. Really."

"I'm always here for you," he said, but the line was already dead.

COLLEEN STRAIGHTENED HER SKIRT AND TOOK ONE LAST glance in the mirror. Her appearance had always been important to her, but only as it extended to her credibility. Neat hair, a simple face of makeup, clothes tidily pressed, these were the things that conveyed to the world that you had it all together. It made people think twice before questioning you.

Now, though... after Ophelia's declaration that one day Colleen would be *magistrate*, not Eugenia, but her, the third child of August Deschanel, she chanced extra looks, double-checking the neatness of her bun, and the soft kohl lines around her eyes. She doubted the others would accept her authority and knew this would be a long game she was playing, to earn their respect.

Their summer meeting was this evening. Colleen puzzled over that, that there'd been no need to call one in between the quarterly schedule, especially with the concern of the Curse being renewed. Had Ophelia ruled that out as a possibility? Had they moved on?

Elizabeth appeared in the doorway and smiled. Colleen smiled back. She'd seen such positive changes in her baby sister, who'd thrived at Ophélie, away from the city and all her demons. Colleen hadn't initially supported her mother's idea to uproot the family, but maybe the idea had merit, after all.

"You have a meeting tonight?"

Colleen nodded. "I do. Why, did you wanna come? Tonight is Council only. There's one for the full Collective in two weeks, and you're old enough now."

Elizabeth chewed the inside of her lip. "I don't know. Sounds stuffy."

Colleen watched her. Elizabeth wasn't worried about a stuffy meeting. Here, she only saw her siblings, mother, and occasionally that strange but sweet Connor. In a room filled with Deschanels, her visions would skyrocket. "Think about it. Being a member of the Collective is your birthright, Lizzy. Sometimes it's nice to remember the world—our world—is bigger than the seven."

"The six," Elizabeth corrected. She shuffled her feet.

"Lizzy..." Colleen looked off in thought. "Mama said something, when we moved here. She said you'd seen Maddy... well, that you'd seen what would happen to her."

Elizabeth stiffened from head to toe. She drew her lips into a tight line. “It wasn’t my fault, Leena.”

“Oh, sweetie, I know that. I know.” Colleen dropped her lipstick and went to Elizabeth. She pressed her hair back off her face. It was always in her face. Unlike Evangeline, whose hair could be tamed by nothing, Elizabeth chose to let hers hang limp around her jaw, like a veil of mourning. “That’s not why I was asking.”

“Why *were* you asking?’

“I shouldn’t be telling you this if you’re not in the Collective...”

“Tell me anyway.”

Colleen pressed her lips together, then rolled the bottom one through her teeth. “There’s talk that maybe the Deschanel Curse is back. It wasn’t only Maddy. We received word of a couple cousins, in France. And some are seeing that as a pattern that indicates something more sinister... something more Deschanel.”

Elizabeth knitted her brows together. Her face scrunched hard, thinking. “That’s why you want me to come? So I can predict more deaths?”

“No,” Colleen said quickly. “I don’t need you to come to the meetings, and I would never ask anything of you that you weren’t comfortable with, but, Lizzy, it’s of my belief that the Curse is perhaps *not* so supernatural. That there may be some deep, scientific link, something obscure maybe, like quantum physics. Hard to understand, but with the right minds...”

“How would you study that? You’d need a mad scientist with a big old lab.”

“We could cross that bridge if we got there,” Colleen replied. “But if I *knew* someone was going to die... there may be things I could watch for. Commonalities. Things we could compare to other deaths that are outside this family. You’ve predicted the deaths of classmates and families that aren’t ours, too, Lizzy. We could compare them.”

“That sounds morbid,” Elizabeth said, crossing her arms. “Even for me.”

“I... yes, I suppose.”

“You’re going to find someone who’s about to die and ask them if you can study them until they kick the bucket? And they're just going to smile and say thanks for letting me be the bunny in your lab in my last days on earth?"

Colleen balked. She wasn't as heartless as what Elizabeth described, even if it did sound that way. "Lizzy, I don't just want to study them. I'm hoping to find a way to change the future. Don't you understand? Everyone says that can't be done, but how many times has it even been attempted? How many people in the world are like you that there's even been enough evidence, or studies, or data that attempting to stop what is confirmed to happen works or doesn't? Most men and women have nothing more than a bad feeling. They might call it a premonition, like someone walking over their grave, but it isn't anywhere near what you can do. You have never predicted anything wrong, Elizabeth. Not once. And it eats you up inside. You have to live with this for the rest of your life, so wouldn't you want to even try to be a part of something that might take your ability and turn it into something positive?"

"The future can't be changed, Colleen. It just can't."

"But how do you know?"

"I know!"

"Yes, but *how*?"

Elizabeth recoiled from her touch. "The same way I know Maddy's death wasn't some Curse. She just died. They all *just die*! But you know what's worse sometimes?"

Colleen said nothing.

"What's worse is knowing what will happen to each of you while you're still living." Elizabeth's eyes trembled in their sockets as she trained them on her older sister for several long seconds. Then she fled, footsteps following her down the hall. A door slammed.

Colleen collapsed back onto her bed. She wanted to follow Elizabeth, to tell her she would go to medical school and prove her wrong, and maybe save her sanity in the process. That there *must* be some other reason they were given such gifts, other than causing harm to themselves and others.

But she was no longer so sure.

CHAPTER 10
I Know What You Did

Red and green ribbons of colors danced through the sky. There were other scientific phenomena that could cause this, but Evangeline tended to favor the theoretical principle of Occam's razor, which said that, all things equal, the simplest solution, or the one with the fewest needed assumptions, was the correct one.

This was Louisiana, in late summer. A storm was coming.

Evangeline hadn't been following the news, but her friend Cassidy had. Promptly on the heels of Evangeline's own assessment of the coming storm, Cassidy bounced in, announcing that the tropical storm meteorologists had been monitoring in the Gulf had been upgraded to a Category 4 Hurricane. The eye would pass right over New Orleans. Evacuation orders were imminent.

She watched in mild bemusement as all the kids, her friends, whipped themselves into a flurry of excitement and panic. They needed to call their parents! To get a sibling out of school! What would they pack? Where would they go?

It wasn't that Evangeline didn't share their concerns. With her limited information, unless the trajectory of the storm shifted, damage was certain. The areas to the north and east of the city center would fare the worst, those rows of little matchstick shotgun cottages housing the poor and working class. The Quarter would need some cleanup, but it was built better, to withstand such things. The Garden District rarely saw any lasting damage. They were the literal and figurative higher ground, if being a few feet above sea level could be considered high ground.

But the Deschanels had never evacuated. Evacuation, for them, was battening the hatches at Ophélie, and now they lived there full-time, so this was as simple, for Evangeline, as going home. Augustus was expecting her back at the office soon. He'd wait for her, and they'd drive home together. No use getting worked up about it when the answer was clear.

One by one, the kids shuffled out of the empty warehouse, filtering off to their families, or homes, or wherever they went when they weren't here. Cassidy hoisted her bag over her shoulder and hovered over where Evangeline lay sprawled on the dirty couch. "You need to beat it, too, Ivy. This place is gonna be a swamp by morning."

"It takes many years and massive ecological change to form a swamp," Evangeline replied. She rested her open comic across her chest.

"Ivy, you're unreal sometimes, you know that?"

Ivy. The name started by accident, when someone misheard her, and then stuck. She didn't correct them. It was better to be more anonymous here than she'd been in her last group, where she was now an anathema. Or worse.

She walked the long way back through the Quarter and into the CBD to avoid running into any of them, and steered at least four blocks clear of Dauphine. Who could say whether their threats were real or not. Evangeline had the odds at 70 percent, and that was higher than she liked.

It had started when Ethan Summerland disappeared in the spring. Some of the kids thought he'd cut town, with the fuzz hot on his operation. No one would have doubted the potential of this, as he dealt to minors and certainly there were other suspect actions happening in his flat on Dauphine.

Not everyone thought this, though. Others had a more sinister view of his absence, eyeing Evangeline with a suspicion she didn't at all understand. Not at first, anyway. Not until Craig, who she'd avoided since the unfortunate loss of her virginity, was good enough to warn her what the whole thing was about.

"You better split, bunny."

"Split? Why?"

He leaned in. He reeked so strongly of pot that Evangeline nearly scored a contact high. "They think your brother did it."

"Did what?"

"You know."

"No, I don't know. I don't know anything, or why everyone is treating me like I stole their grass."

Craig looked around, then returned to her, wide-eyed. "Ethan. They think he took care of Ethan the way he took care of that teacher."

Evangeline's head shook. She couldn't focus on all these strange, disconnected bombshells Craig seemed to be so certain about. "What? What teacher? What are you talking about?"

He lowered his voice. "Everyone knows Charles whacked that teacher who was jumping your sister's bones."

"That's not true, and you need to stop repeating that shit," Evangeline hissed. "That never happened."

Craig shrugged and she wanted to beat the grin from his scruffy face. "It's copacetic, sister. All I'm saying is, my buddy Jared is the one who gave him the info about that English teacher boning your little sis." He snapped his fingers. "Shit, I know his name. It was all over the papers... you know, the dude who taught Shakespeare... Anders... Avery... Elway... damn it, it's right on the tip of my tongue..."

Evers. The blood drained away from Evangeline's face, and she was suddenly hot, just absolutely on fire. How many times had the police been over to the house to question Maureen? And every time, Colleen and Augustus hovered around her, watching her closely.

Evangeline had thought they were protecting her, but had they been coaching her?

No. Charles would never.

"Craig, mind your business. Gossip is for old women in sewing circles," she snapped, but her mind was working, working around this new development, this new hitch in the plot. "Besides, Charles has bought coke from Ethan. He wouldn't ruin a good thing."

"Unless he thought that good thing was ruining his little sister," Craig said wisely, and she walked completely away from him then, without another word.

Could it be true? Could Charles really be playing God behind the scenes, flexing his muscles to keep his sisters safe? She'd studied enough of the true crime sections in the newspaper to know that trouble often started at home. Occam's razor worked especially well in solving murders.

But how could Craig, whose last name she didn't even *know*, be so sure of something that Evangeline had never even considered? How had she never heard any of this?

She should have heeded his warning sooner. The threats started as whispers as people passed by her, but then one of the girls, one of Ethan's favorites, cornered her late at night on a side street, with a switchblade. Serenity, she was called, but that wasn't her real name. Evangeline never learned it.

"We know what your brother did to Ethan." Serenity's hot breath burned her ears. Spittle dotted her flesh. "Bring a thousand dollars tomorrow or we'll slit you tits to ass."

It was then Evangeline realized there were others, hovering in the shadows. Evangeline wasn't afraid of one girl, switchblade or no, but she had no bravado about the odds of winning a fight against multiple assailants.

Evangeline avoided going the next day, but they found her instead. She'd been fetching lunch for herself and Augustus down on Canal when Serenity popped up behind her.

"We haven't forgotten, and you're a day late. We know who

your family is, and where to find them. Now, it's two thousand. Tomorrow night."

Evangeline knew where to find the cash. Her mother socked it away in lumps throughout the house, and Evangeline had simply narrowed down the odds of where those places might be by assessing the known variables. The compartment holding the money must be small, but the place of hiding bigger, to avoid suspicion. She would not put it anywhere the kids would find it, but it also could not be anywhere as obvious as her underwear drawer.

The stash had been peppered into canisters of the food that no one in the house dared eat. Oats, Tang, Spam. Evangeline found over twenty thousand dollars stashed away in forgotten food, so she knew exactly where to go, to pay off Serenity's extortion.

What other choice did she have? She ticked down the list of options as the two thousand dollars burned a hole in her jeans pocket.

She could let Serenity murder her. Selfless, but not ideal.

She could not go into town anymore, until everything died down. Not practical, and Serenity had inferred a threat against Evangeline's siblings as an alternative.

She could tell Charles and let the chips fall where they may. But she couldn't even fathom that Charles might have already killed for them, and she might never sleep again if she confirmed it with her own request for help.

Or she could pay Serenity and hope this went away.

Even Evangeline knew that was unlikely, but she wouldn't put her family in danger, and she wasn't really cool about being murdered herself.

Serenity took the money from Evangeline's shaking hands with a nasty grin. "Smashing." Her eyes glittered with excitement as she flipped through the stack of bills. "Now we want four."

"Four thousand?" Evangeline repeated. "Come on, I gave you what you wanted."

Serenity ran the cold steel blade, which was half-rusted now that Evangeline could see it closer, a fact that made the situation worse, for she calculated the increase in pain that would result in a faulty knife. They couldn't even confront her with a proper weapon. "And you'll keep doing it until we say otherwise."

Two. Four. Ten. Fifteen. Evangeline went through the motions, until she was nearly out of her mother's secret stash. Never mind that Irish Colleen would eventually, maybe soon, notice the cash missing. But where would Evangeline get more when it was gone?

When they asked for fifteen, and Evangeline had less than half that left from the food stash, she accepted that this arrangement was no longer sustainable. This also meant her personal danger was great.

Cassidy would never know she'd saved Evangeline. Cassidy was one of Ethan's groupies, but had peeled away before he disappeared. She ran into Evangeline as she was leaving the dangerous group one night and seemed genuinely happy to see her.

"Please tell me you're not still hanging with Ethan's crew," Cassidy said in a low voice.

Evangeline shrugged.

"Come with me." Cassidy smiled and tugged at her arm. "A bunch of us got away and made our own crew. You can call us Life After Ethan, but really we just like to hang and be cool and not worry about anything. Chill out, smoke out. You know."

"Yeah," Evangeline said. "Cool."

"Well, you're good people, Ivy, so you're in. That is your name, right? Ivy?"

Evangeline had nodded, because she was nothing if not adaptable, and anonymity was safer.

"And don't worry. None of his asshole friends know about this place. You're safe from his controlling."

"Don't you know? He's gone. Disappeared."

Cassidy laughed. "Let's hope it lasts."

That was a month ago, and Evangeline still didn't really know any of the kids in Life After Ethan, and she was good with that.

"I gotta go. My mom is going to be flipping her wig," Cassidy said, shooting furtive looks at the door where the last of the kids filtered out. "She can give you a ride, you know."

"It's cool. I'll get one from my brother."

"If you're sure..."

"I'm sure."

Cassidy blew her a kiss and skipped out of the old warehouse. The last one out, except Evangeline.

Outside, the rain started. It didn't mean much, only that the outer bands were active. No danger yet. Evangeline checked her watch. Augustus would be out of class in thirty minutes, which meant he would be at the office in just under an hour. The locks were in now, so she couldn't come and go without him anymore. He'd meant to make her a key, but they'd both forgotten, and so she just timed her arrivals with his.

Evangeline closed her eyes. The room was devoid of sound other than the light mechanical clicks and clunks from the buildings nearby. She could think of so few times in her life when the world around her had been truly quiet.

She awoke to cold steel pressing into the soft flesh of her neck. Her pulse throbbed, and each movement was a pierce of pain.

"You didn't think we'd find you?" Serenity said. "You don't get to blow us off, Deschanel. We don't just go away."

"I don't have any more money," Evangeline managed, through the pressure on her windpipe. She was afraid to move... she understood there was no room for error.

Serenity made a little *hmph* noise that was almost sweet. With her free hand, she signaled. A shuffling of feet came next, and then Evangeline saw, through her limited view, three men appear in the arc of her vision. She knew two of them.

"If you don't have money, then we'll take what you do have," Serenity said.

THE TAXI SEAT WAS COLD, WHICH SHOULD HAVE BEEN soothing against the bruises on the back of her thighs. It wasn't.

The smell of the old, peeling plastic made her nauseated, and she nearly threw up. Only the absence of anything left to vomit stopped her.

The taxi driver checked three times with her if she didn't want to stop at a hospital instead. She didn't trust him, either, didn't trust anyone anymore, not him, not her brother, not anyone. He was likely more concerned with being pulled into an investigation than anything else, and Evangeline had nothing left for him.

"No. I want to go home," she said, and he reminded her that a taxi all the way to Vacherie was going to cost a lot more than she probably had.

Evangeline still had the last of the money she'd stolen from her mother in her knapsack. Amazingly, Serenity and her friends hadn't thought to look there after... after...

"You don't know what I have." *And you don't know what I've lost.*

The tears dried up by the time the I-10 turned into I-310. But the pain was not as forgiving. She sat sideways in the bench seat, her legs bowed outward. She said a silent prayer, though she didn't believe in God, that she wouldn't leave blood behind for the taxi driver to clean up. Not to do him any favors. The thought of evidence of that night might exist anywhere else horrified her.

He didn't say another word the rest of the ride, though his eyes traveled to her bloodied, huddled form in the rearview. He wanted to ask. He didn't.

EVANGELINE SLIPPED INTO SWEATS AND A HEAVY sweater after her short bath. She craved the cleanliness of the water, but she couldn't bear the pain for long. She washed off as much of the night as she could manage, and then hobbled to her room.

"Evangeline?"

Colleen's voice. Why was she addressing her? Colleen hated her. Had hated her since the incident with Rory.

"Where have you been? Augustus was worried sick. You were

supposed to come home with him." She pointed to the window at the end of the hall. "There's a hurricane coming, you know."

Evangeline winced as she released the handle of the door. How could Colleen not know, not sense her suffering? Had they drifted so far apart?

"I don't want to talk tonight," Evangeline said without turning.

"You never do, when someone wants to hold you accountable." Colleen stepped closer, and Evangeline cringed, curling into a standing fetal position. "I know who you've been hanging out with."

The tears took Evangeline by surprise. She'd thought they were dried up, like whatever else inside her made her human. "Not tonight, Colleen."

"Ethan Summerland. Evangeline, you're smarter than this."

Evangeline winced as the pain buckled her knees. "Please, leave me alone."

"Whatever happened between us, I'm still your sister. I don't want to see something happen to you."

Yeah? Too late, Colleen.

Evangeline forced herself to stand straight. Her head turned, and the spot where the knife had broken the surface of her neck screamed at her. "Talk to Charles, then. Ask him what happened to Ethan Summerland."

She rushed through the door and locked it behind her, safe, finally.

No, not safe. She'd be safer outside, in the coming storm.

She'd never be truly safe again.

FALL 1972

VACHERIE, LOUISIANA
NEW ORLEANS, LOUISIANA

CHAPTER 11

Prepare For the Worst

The envelope didn't look like much. Plain and white, with nothing printed on the outside to suggest the interesting contents within. Only the return address—Scotland—betrayed the potential.

Potential was all it was for the time being. The packet contained the information Colleen had been waiting weeks for: a brochure singing the benefits of the medical program at the University of Edinburgh, and an invitation to submit up to two years out.

The timing was right. Colleen had just started her third year of undergrad in New Orleans and would need to make decisions soon. That she was determined to go to medical school wasn't up for debate, but *where* was.

There were other schools in the stack. Johns Hopkins, Stanford, Yale, Case Western. Applying to any of these was pointless; if she wanted in, she'd get in. She was a great, but not exceptional, student, but a Deschanel would never have to knock hard to open any door.

But Scotland was different. The Deschanel name didn't carry as much weight in Europe, outside of France, and something about the rolling green hills of the Highlands called to her in a way nothing else ever had. Colleen didn't romanticize much in life, but her notions of what this ancient land held in store for her were the height of romance, inducing a side of her she was surprised to learn existed.

It was away from New Orleans and her responsibilities, but she'd begun to wonder if she might lead this family better with some space first. None of her siblings except Augustus wanted anything to do with her. They couldn't see through their anger at her perceived meddling to understand *why* she stepped up and made the family business her own.

An hour later, Colleen dropped the completed application in the outgoing mail stack. As an afterthought she slipped it into the middle of the pile. She felt dirty, somehow, like even putting in the application was an act of betrayal. The sting was only somewhat lessened by the knowledge her siblings, and maybe even her mother, would be glad to be rid of her for a while.

All the phones in the house started ringing. They stopped after the first ring, before she could answer the one in the downstairs office. Soon after, Condoleezza came shuffling down the stairs at a pace faster than Colleen had ever seen the woman move.

"Colleen, thank goodness! You're still here!"

"I was on my way to class. What's going on? What's wrong?"

Their head housekeeper shook her head and kept shaking it. "Child, you need to get yourself to Charity Hospital. Miss Ophelia has taken down with pneumonia, and at her age, that might not be ailing her long."

Colleen's heart seized in her chest. Condoleezza was still talking, something about Blanche and Eugenia, but she couldn't pull her focus around the words. Ophelia was in the hospital, and she wasn't ready for this. She wasn't anywhere near ready, hadn't done a thing to prepare herself, and now the moment was upon her.

The housekeeper excused herself and returned moments later with an amber pan filled with cake. "Take this, child. For Blanche. It isn't much, but it's what I've got on short notice."

Colleen nodded. She didn't remember accepting the pan, but noted that it was in her arms, with her cardigan.

She'd never put much faith in signs, but she couldn't ignore the timing of this news, just as she'd been daydreaming of leaving all this behind.

One day, a day that will not be so very far in the future, you'll be sitting in my chair, Colleen. You'll be leading this family...

"I'll find your mama and she can get the rest of the children down there. Lord can pray it won't be too late." Condoleezza crossed herself and scuttled off, as quickly as she'd made her appearance.

COLLEEN EMBRACED HER AUNT BLANCHE WITH TWO brief kisses. Blanche, who, even at home, always wore her Sunday church dresses, looked as if she were late for a ladies' luncheon, if not for the heavy rim of red around her eyes.

"She's stable now, God bless, but we all know this can't go on forever." Blanche dabbed at her eyes. "Eugenia and Wallace said they'd move into The Gardens to see after her, but the tomb of a dying woman is no place for children."

"Now, Mama, that's a touch dramatic, don't you think? My boys love their Tant*e*." Eugenia appeared beside her mother, slipping her arm around her tiny waist. "Hi, Colleen. It's good of you to come."

Blanche pulled a satin handkerchief from the waist pocket of her paisley dress and sniffed. She had always been a picture, and still was, now in her sixties. She'd left behind more broken hearts than she'd satisfied, with her first two husbands dead under mysterious circumstances. Colleen always remembered this fact, above all others, when she thought of Blanche, whose cold eyes regarded the world behind her spidery lashes and neat appearances.

"My mother and the others may be on their way as well," Colleen replied, though she didn't know if they were, or if they loved Aunt Ophelia as she did. Many in the family thought her an old kook and paid little mind to her.

That wasn't entirely true. Evangeline loved her, too, and

Colleen knew her sister was home when the call came in. She should have taken her.

"She's given us a scare, but the doctors say she'll only be here a few nights," Eugenia said pleasantly. "Tante Ophelia is a tough old bird. It will take more than this to knock her down."

"Is she awake or resting?"

Eugenia smiled. "Supposed to be resting, but we both know how she felt about that order."

Colleen nodded at them both and moved past them in a daze, toward the room. Nurses rushed past her, going about their business, as if the matriarch of New Orleans was not among their many patients. Machines beeped. The competing scents of disinfectant and cigarette smoke were so strong they almost broke her from her stupor. Pierce and Cassius huddled nearby, and both looked up to acknowledge her, then returned to their thoughts.

Colleen slipped past a nurse exiting her aunt's room. The smell of smoke grew overwhelming when she stepped in, and she realized, with horror, that Ophelia was smoking.

"You have pneumonia!" Colleen cried. She rushed to her aunt's bedside and tried to take the offensive thing, but her aunt leveled her with a hard look.

"At my age I can have pneumonia and still enjoy my vices," she rasped. "And you won't do a thing to stop me, Colleen Deschanel."

Colleen gasped lightly at the rebuke. She settled into a chair by the bed and didn't attempt it again, but she made her disgust known by waving the smoke from the air. "You'll kill yourself doing that."

"And if I do, I'll still have outlived almost every last Deschanel on record." She erupted in a coughing fit. When she was done, her yellow smile appeared through the smoke. "Look that up for me in your research, will you? I do believe I am a bona fide record-breaker. I can't die without knowing."

"You might if—"

"Yes, yes. You've made your point, Colleen. That isn't why you came to see me, though."

"I thought you were dying!"

"Well, I am, child. I'm ninety-four, for the love of Christ." Her shaking hand brought the ash-laden cigarette to her lips and she drew a deep drag. "Just not today."

Colleen's breath hitched as her emotions caught up. "You make jokes about something that isn't funny. It isn't funny at all."

"It's my choice whether the subject of my own death brings me comic relief, is it not? Have I not earned that?"

"Tante!"

Ophelia's phlegm-filled laugh was more cough than humor. "You're cross with me again, but I can't fathom the reason. I gave you my greatest advice, and you've not followed it a whit."

"What do you mean? I've tried to make things right at home… I've given up on Rory. What else was I supposed to be doing?"

"Half-hearted attempts at both, and at most," Ophelia replied. "But I'll not be cross with you in return, Colleen. It is, after all, your life. Your choice. One can make mistakes once or a thousand times, that is the beauty of choice, if one sees beauty in such a malformed light."

"I didn't come here to talk about me, Tante."

"No?"

"I came because I was terrified for you."

"And, as you can see with your eyes, I'm still breathing and making my own choices. Still possessed of all, or most, of my faculties."

"Why do you joke about these things?" Tears tickled her cheeks.

"It's healthier than obsessing over the inevitable. I've been waiting to die my whole life, and here I am."

"Have you seen it?"

"What, child?"

"Your death. In your visions."

Ophelia transferred the cigarette to her other hand. She patted Colleen's. "You won't tease such information out of me, no matter how you go about it," she said, but was smiling.

"But have you?"

"I won't ever say!" she declared. "But since you are in a state, and I know you won't let this go, I'll tell you I *did* see your father's death. And I told him about it."

"Why?"

Ophelia's eyes closed for several long seconds. The wrinkled flesh fluttered open again. "Because what has been seen cannot be changed. And I was fully aware my nephew had two daughters at home, capable healers, who would blame themselves when they failed to save him. I wanted him to spare you this agony."

"But..." Colleen puzzled over the right words. "His cancer *was* curable by a healer."

Ophelia nodded. "Except I'd already scryed his future, and his future was set in stone. His future was one where he opted not to be healed."

"That's a circular argument! If you hadn't told him this, he would have let us heal him and would have lived."

"No, child, because in the future I saw his fate had already been determined."

Colleen shot out of her seat. She could hardly breathe, for all the deception and pretty language. "And *this,* Tante, is why I will go to college and study what we are. I'll study death and premonitions, and I'll prove that the future *can* be changed."

"And you'll be wasting your time," her aunt said evenly. "Yet you'll do it nonetheless."

"I won't apologize for trusting science over instinct."

"I'd never expect such a thing from you."

"You're taunting me."

"No," Ophelia said. "Simply pointing out a truth we are both already painfully aware of."

Colleen fled from the room while her aunt was still talking; still spewing the nonsense Colleen thought she was above, and immune to. She didn't know if it was senility, regret, fear, or something else, but the woman in that room was not the one she'd sought out for counsel so many times over the years.

Cassius called after her, and then Eugenia followed suit, but she raced past them. Blanche's darlings could hover there in concern, happily oblivious, but Colleen could not. Could not, could not, could not.

When she came to the stairs, she raced down so fast she lost a shoe. She reached down to retrieve it when she felt the presence of another.

Rory, in his trench coat.

Rory, love on his face.

Rory.

Always Rory.

Ophelia was wrong about this, as she was wrong about so many other things.

Colleen fell into his arms and sobbed.

Maureen had never found much interest in her family history. She knew her ancestor, Charles, emigrated from France sometime in the middle of the 1800s, built Ophélie, and was involved in some exciting scandals during and after the Civil War. But she could not have named any of his children. She didn't know how many generations existed between this ancestor and herself, or anything that had happened in the years between. History, to her, was about as useful as clothes that no longer fit, or food that had spoiled. What was then would never again be now, and there was no use paying it any mind.

Now, she knew about the entire sordid ordeal. She'd guess she might know more, even, than that decrepit relic Ophelia, or Colleen. Could they say they'd heard the stories from the people who lived them?

No. They weren't freaks like her.

Jean, the oldest son of Charles, spent his days telling his story, over and over. Of how his mother, Brigitte, put everything on sustaining the family bloodline. Maureen didn't pay this much mind in the beginning. She was too distracted by his strange way of dressing and unusual inflections of speech. But she perked right up when she finally understood his meaning.

Brigitte had ordered her children to make a child of their own.

Maureen began paying attention in spite of herself. Jean was a monster. No matter how he tried to justify his own depraved actions, of insisting his repeated rapes of his younger sister, Ophélie, being a matter of honor, it was clear he enjoyed the tasks assigned to him with the fervor of a genuine sociopath. She'd never admit this to anyone, and supposed she'd never have to in any case, but there was something almost thrilling about listening to him speak of how he'd snuck into his sister's room... of the relish in the terror dancing in her eyes. How he performed his duty, night after night. Maureen's own fantasies weren't nearly as terrible, but they had always been taboo. She didn't know, but she supposed that made her a monster, too.

Jean rambled, day in and day out, like a man possessed. Fitz, the youngest of Brigitte and Charles' children, was also there. Unlike the calculated, poised Jean, Fitz seemed a man who had lived, and died, half stuck in his own imagination. He spent his days flitting about her room, wondering at her old dolls or her makeup. He talked of the books he'd read.

The abused sister, Ophélie, never did appear. Maureen hoped that meant she'd found a way to find peace and move on.

Jean's son, Charles II, was a somber, lumbering fellow who even in death had not shrugged off his serious gravitas. So far, Maureen's ghosts hadn't come with any scent, but she imagined him smelling of old cigars and rotting wood. He told her he was her grandfather, and what a weird revelation that was! Her friends talked about their grandparents like fairies bearing gifts and joy, but she'd never known any of her grandparents. She knew only that her father's parents died long before he had his first child. She knew nothing about her mother's family.

"Grandpa," she said, marveling at how the word sounded in her mouth.

"I didn't live long enough to see August deliver on his legacy," said the behemoth Charles. "He had to go and wed that Yankee and throw his honor to the wind."

"Eliza?" Maureen knew very little about his father's first wife, only that he'd married her for love and she'd died childless.

"We don't give names to traitors."

Maureen did some nominal math in her head and determined he must have been born not long after the war, when people still actually called people Yankees in earnest and meant it as a dire indictment.

"Don't listen to my father." August appeared very rarely when Charles II was lurking about. There was a tension between them, bordering on resentment, teetering on hatred. "He was from a much older generation, where they didn't understand happiness comes from things other than doing what's expected."

She wondered what her grandfather would think of her Virgins Only club. The thought amused her and also made her long for a time when she'd had enough freedom to make decisions like this. She knew now that what she'd done with those boys was foolish, but in her own way, she missed it. Missed the thrill of standing on old metal bars and commanding them to her whim. Of knowing she was taking something from them that someone had taken from her, but also freeing them from the bondage imposed by the arbitrary threads of childhood.

But she'd be lying if she said she didn't miss some of those threads. Irish Colleen had begun their homeschooling and didn't know a thing about any of what she was supposed to be teaching. She struggled to read half the curriculum, and often left the girls alone to read it themselves and then summarize back to her, as if they didn't see right through the motivation. Maureen never thought she'd miss her dry public school teachers, but she did. If one had to go to school, they should at least get a semblance of an education out of it.

She missed her friends, even Chelsea. The boys she'd bedded, who later eyed her in the halls as if she were a great queen, or maybe a mafia don. She missed the sound of hundreds of voices in the halls, and the hustle and bustle of the schoolyard.

Instead, she rotted away in this ancient family home, surrounded by the ghosts of those who had made the family infamous.

Pansy's ceremony was supposed to rid Maureen of her ghosts; instead, they screamed louder, and there were so many more. Not only Jean, Fitz, and Charles II, but also servants who had died in suspicious ways; children who never made it to adults. The high-pitched screams of her father's three siblings, who had died as toddlers from yellow fever, never dulled, even in the middle of the night. While the rest of the house slept, Maureen had to listen to John, Jean, and Elizabeth call out for their maman and papa.

The only reprieve, if one could call it that, was that, for reasons she'd never understood, her ghosts had less staying power at Ophélie. They spent their energy more quickly, always had. As with everything else, she had no one to ask.

When Maureen called Pansy to tell her what her magic had wrought, Pansy told her that magic was unpredictable. "Voodoo gives us what we need, sometimes more so than what we want."

What a load of crud! How could this life be what she needed?

"If I could make them go away, I would," Madeline said. She peered at her from the pillow on the other side of the bed. No creases appeared where she lay. The side was untouched by anything real.

"I would make you go away if I could," Maureen said, but the words formed a lump in her throat. "I'm sorry, Maddy. I don't mean it."

"I know what you mean," Madeline said. She didn't sound in death as she had in life. In life, Madeline had been in constant torment from absorbing the pain of the world around her. In death, she was at peace, but there was still a darkness around her, of a life unlived, and of things undone. "I wish I could say I'd be more helpful to you if I was still alive, but I don't think I would. I didn't realize how little of my own family's pain I was ignorant about until I was free of the pain. And yet... I knew about you and that teacher, and I chose to keep that to myself."

"What? How?"

Madeline shrugged. "You weren't as clever about the secret as you thought. Mama prides herself on her instincts, but she never did learn about this, did she?"

"Don't think so," Maureen muttered. She made the mistake of looking in Mr. Evers' direction, and he asked the usual question. She pulled the covers tight over her head.

"I have so many regrets," Madeline said. Her voice was soft, whimsical, but also sad, and Maureen knew what would come next. "If I had known what would happen, I would have done things so differently, Maureen."

"That's how life works. We die, and things are left the way they're left."

"Most people don't die before they're an adult."

Maureen groaned. "Tell that to the Three Stooges howling for their mom."

"Who?"

"You can't hear them?"

Madeline directed her eyes to the side and listened. "I can, now that you've said it. It's weird like that. I can't see your other ghosts until you've told me about them."

Maureen let the covers slip a little. Her head peeked all the way out. "Really?"

"I didn't hear the children until you talked about them. And I didn't know that your dead teacher was here until you threw a glass at him. Why is he here, Maureen?"

"Charles killed him," Maureen said, with no more interest than she'd give a conversation about the change in weather. "And now he won't leave me alone."

Madeline's eyes went wide. "I didn't know he had it in him."

"Me neither, but you know what they say about murder."

"What?"

"Once you get a taste for it, it's all over. Murderer for life."

Madeline looked skeptical. "Do they say that? Who's they?"

"You know. They."

"So you think Charles has murdered people before your teacher? Or after?"

"How should I know?" Maureen was annoyed by the conversation suddenly. "Who else can you see?" She prayed Madeline could not hear the baby. This would be of no relief, to share this burden. It would only amplify how terrible things could get.

"Let's see... your teacher, now the kids. I can see Dad, which..." Madeline's eyes glistened. "I never thought I'd see him again, and it's almost more than I can take. And I can also see an old man you call Charles."

"Yeah. Our grandpa."

"Grandpa." Madeline wore a look of pure wonder that matched how Maureen felt, every now and then, at these strange, though unwelcome, glimpses into her past. "I think that's it."

"There's also Jean and Fitz, but you're not missing much."

"Mind your tongue," Jean snapped from the corner. "I'm your elder."

Maureen didn't address him directly. She wouldn't give him the satisfaction of a broader audience.

"That's just bonkers," Madeline said, shaking her head. "Who else knows about this?"

"No one. And I want to keep it that way."

"Do you think there's anyone else who can help you? Someone who isn't Pansy?"

Maureen wasn't going to take any more risks. Pansy's "help" had turned her life into a veritable zoo of the dead. What if the next person made her see *all* the dead people, like a bad zombie movie?

When Maureen didn't answer, Madeline went on. "Have you always been able to see Daddy? Since he died?"

"I don't want to talk about this anymore."

"I know we weren't always close—"

"When you were alive but should be now that you're dead?" Maureen finished. Her laugh was clipped. "I don't need friends, Maddy. I need peace and quiet!"

"Why, Maureen?" Like clockwork came the refrain.

"I'm only saying, you're not the only one who has secrets. I know you don't completely believe I'm here, but I could tell you something… something only I and one other person know, that you could confirm with them as proof."

"As far as I'm concerned, you died with your secrets. Don't put that on me." She wasn't talking to the dead. Entertaining them fed them and their power over her. And the deeper, scarier truth was, she couldn't be completely certain that all of this wasn't a figment of her strange imagination. The lack of confirmation was a comfort. As long as she didn't know, there was still a chance her life might turn out normal.

"That's not fair." Quietly, she added, "We'll figure this out, Maureen. I'll help you."

Maureen flipped herself around and buried her face in the pillow. Somewhere, a baby cried, one she had not been able to save, and who would let her know it the remainder of her days. "No, I was alone then and I'm alone now. If fair had anything to do with it, I'd be the happy one."

CHAPTER 12

A Careful Dance of Words and Intentions

In every relationship, there were carefully orchestrated give and takes designed to preserve the health of the bond. A careful dance of words and intentions. Charles had always known the ways to keep Colin happy, and most involved providing the illusion of Colin's superior advice and authority on most matters.

It helped that Colin *was* often right. Or maybe it was more that he was determined to always do the right thing, which was maddening to Charles, but there was something strangely simple about the choice to do what was right. The few times Charles had taken this path, he'd forgone the agony of the decision, and the anguish of the consequences, not that he had ever truly been accountable for any of his misdeeds. But he could understand the appeal to others.

His friendship with Colin had been fractured since summer, though they'd begun to slowly put the pieces back together. The breakup with Cat, which had not smoothed over after all—she was apparently far more stubborn than he'd given her credit for—had Colin seeking out old comforts with Charles. Charles suspected Colin found some of his happiness in being smarter and a better man than Charles, like a thin woman having a fat friend to pad her self-image. But that was an unfair generalization, because Colin loved him like a brother and had dealt with far more from Charles than other men would.

Charles hadn't seen Cat at all, even though she was officially on the market, but their late night clandestine phone calls, almost every night, sustained him. No one knew. No one could know. And he hadn't done anything wrong. Talking wasn't a crime.

Getting to know Cat had changed him. Listening to her idealistic way of seeing the world had fluffed up his own inner Samaritan. He saw a future that called to him and made him believe, even temporarily, that there was a way he could have a life with someone like Catherine Connelly. He'd never had anyone see him through hopeful eyes. Charles would never suffer in life because of who he was born to be, but would also never thrive for the man he'd become. To Cat, he was more than the sum of his dishonorable parts.

What she believed, and what was truth, were not exactly in synch, though. She could believe the best in Charles all day, but at some point the thin threads connecting her hopefulness would snap and fray, unless he stepped up to the image. And if there was anyone who would know how to do that, it was Colin.

The irony was not lost on Charles, who was rarely in the mood to appreciate anything requiring an appreciation of nuance.

Colin listened to him with a blank expression all throughout lunch, as he tried, perhaps not so credibly, to convince his friend that he was serious about turning his life around. The first step, he said, was getting back into college.

Colin's demeanor was one of mounting suspicion. "Okay, but why? Why do you want to go back to school? As you said, you don't have to. There's no stipulation in the estate about the heir requiring an education. You have *no* intention to actually work a day in your life, as I understand it. So why?"

So your ex-girlfriend will see me as a suitable husband. "Sure, okay, you're right. It will be a cold day in hell before I set foot in an office when I'm not a client."

"I'm missing the part where this makes sense, Charles. Let's not forget you spent six years in college and picked up enough credits for, what, two?"

"Almost three."

Colin shook his head. "So?"

"So maybe I don't want to be seen as the lazy heir."

Colin's mouth twitched as he worked to hide a smile. "Why do you care what people think? Or, why *now*? I've known you since we were toddlers, Charles, and you've never cared a whit what anyone thought of the way you lived your life. What's changed?"

"Does it matter?"

"If you want my help, it does."

There was no way Charles could tell the whole truth, but he didn't want to lie, either, not to Colin. There was a partial truth he could share, however, and it was one Colin might even understand and find sympathy in. "I'm getting older and starting to see the future. Mama wants to marry me off, probably to some stuffy bitch, and I'm not going to get any fucking say in the matter."

Colin's arms, crossed over his chest, slackened, then dropped to his sides. "I don't see what that has to do with school. There are other ways to find some control in your life."

Charles shrugged. To increase the probability of belief, he couldn't seem as changed as he felt. "Who the fuck knows? Maybe nothing. Maybe everything. Maybe just a way to wipe the knowing grin off my mother's face. To surprise her by doing exactly the opposite of what she expects of me."

Colin laughed. "Of all the motivations for a college degree, this has to be the most unique."

Charles slumped back in the red leather booth. His arms spread against the back of the seat, hands upturned. "So, will you help me?'

Colin blew out a breath. "I don't think the firm has the muscle you're hoping for. But I can give you advice."

"Advice? What good is that?"

"You have a better chance of getting back into college if *you* deal with this problem instead of delegating it out. You want back in? Talk to the dean, *yourself*. Don't send someone else in. You do it.

You sit and talk to him, face-to-face, and apologize, and then tell him what you'll do differently."

Charles scowled. "Are you serious? Does that fucking sound like something I'd do?"

"You shouldn't ask for my help if you don't want it."

"I do want it, but that's not what I had in mind."

"Do you want back in or not?"

"Yes, but—"

Colin reached into his wallet and pulled out a five. He threw it on the table and stood. "Then I'm telling you, this is the only way to do it. The only thing more powerful than your money is your honor, Charles."

"Where are you going?"

Colin checked his watch. "I'll get to class early, I suppose."

"I have a better idea," Charles replied. He replaced Colin's cash with his own, ignoring Colin's sigh. "Come with me."

Colin's arms crossed again. "I'm not doing this for you."

"No, but I want you there to celebrate with me when I prove all the assholes wrong about me."

Colin sighed, nodded, and followed.

CHARLES HAD RARELY BEEN SO FURIOUS THAT HIS VISION blurred, but as he stormed through the hall, toward the bright light shining beyond the double doors, he could hardly see anything. His heartbeat pounded through the back of his eyes, and the ringing in his ears made everything around him muted and distant.

He shoved the doors open with his fists and waited for them to fly open before marching out into the fall sunshine. He didn't immediately see Colin, and was relieved, because he couldn't deal with his friend's self-righteous *I-told-you-sos,* not when this whole fucking fiasco had been his brilliant idea.

And that fucking dean, with his receding hairline and liver spots. Fucking useless, sad sack of shit.

Charles, I appreciate what it took for you to come see me. I know it wasn't easy for you.

Sure, sure. Is it too late for me to get in for fall term?

The old man folded his gnarled hands together, as if preparing to lead them in prayer. He cleared his throat. *As I said, I appreciate the gesture. But Tulane will not be accepting you back into any of our programs, not now or ever.*

Why the fuck not? Do you know how much money my family has given over the years in... gifts, or whatever the fuck they're called?

Endowments. And yes, I'm exceptionally well aware, as that money has helped us to do many important things. Grow our research facility, for one. But we do not exchange donations for favors, as your mother knows. She has continued to support us in spite of that.

Checks from my fucking money!

A choice, then, that you'll have to make. My decision stands.

Could he really be faulted for assailing the room with the contents of the dean's desk? A paperweight shaped like an apple shattered the glass window behind the old man. A shower of pens, pencils, paper, folders, and other useless shit littered the floor.

No need to call security, you useless fuck, said Charles as the man, wide-eyed and trembling, reached for the phone. *You couldn't pay me to spend another minute in this fucking place.*

Colin jogged over from where he'd been waiting on the bench. "That was quick. How did it go?"

"Fuck this place," Charles said and blew past him. "Let's see how these pricks operate without my millions."

"That answers that," Colin muttered as he struggled to keep pace. "What happened?"

"What do you think happened?"

"I gather he said no, but what did you do?"

Charles came to an abrupt halt in the grass. He spun on Colin. "Why do you always assume the problem is me?"

"I wonder if it's anything to do with how much you *are* the problem?" Colin started to roll his eyes, then thought better of it. "Your temper gets the best of you all the time. Too often."

“Why should I have to bend over for the world?”

Colin glanced around the courtyard. Probably wondering if others were looking, if they were drawing attention, because he was always concerned about stupid things like that. “That you would even ask the question in that way is part of the problem, Charles.”

“I guess it would be better to be more like you, is that it? To be a fucking robot who can’t even hold onto his girl because he’s so much better than everyone else?”

Colin paled in an instant. His entire demeanor changed. “You know *nothing* about that. About her.” He rolled his wrist to check his watch, but his eyes were elsewhere, distant. “Why do you even ask me what I think?”

Charles sputtered a few attempts at an answer. “You’re right, asking you never fucking works out for me.”

“That’s not—”

Charles pulled the pack of smokes from his shirt, lit one, and inhaled a long drag. “No, no, you’re on to something, my friend. There’s a pattern of me coming to you for advice, and the advice you give being fucking terrible. You told me to forget about my own daughter.”

“That’s not what—”

Charles took another heavy drag. “Oh yes, and the *many* times you encouraged me not to cheat on a test, and then I failed anyway.”

Colin was flabbergasted. “Because you never studied!”

“Does the reason matter?”

“Yes!”

“And now, you tell me to go in there, be a man, own up to my actions.” Two streams of smoke poured from his nose. “I nearly get thrown out by security.”

Colin’s head shook in disbelief. “I don’t even know how to argue with your twisted logic.”

Charles pointed the cigarette at him. “Because I’m right.”

“No!” Colin screamed the word, and people gathered around in the grass looked over. “No, you’re not right! You’re never right! And I’m sick and tired of trying to be the sane one in this relationship, and of having my friendship thrown back in my face when things don't turn out the way you want them, which, of course, is because you are constantly screwing your life up!"

Charles blew out his laugh through his smoke.

Colin threw his hands in the air. "I'm done! I'm not going to babysit you anymore, because even if I wanted to spend the effort, you're beyond help!"

"You always say shit like that."

"Yeah?" This time, Colin did note the time from his watch. "Be careful, one day I'll mean it."

He hoisted his bookbag over one shoulder and took off across the quad.

Charles didn't start the day intending to end it the way he *now* intended, but Colin had no one but himself to blame.

He jogged over to a payphone and reached into his wallet. He knew the number by heart, but small deceptions helped form the bigger ones. If he didn't know her number by heart, he could pretend he'd never thought about making this call.

Cat answered on the second ring. "Huck!" she cried, and his knees buckled. "We never talk during the day. Everything okay?"

"Are you alone?"

She breathed in and paused. "Until Monday. Jeannie is ditching classes to go to Destin with Harry, even though I told her it's a terrible idea."

"How terrible of an idea? More terrible than me coming over?"

"Huck..."

"Tell me not to."

She sighed, and he could swear he heard her smiling. "I can't tell you no."

"You can't or won't?"

A small sound on her end made his heart skip. "Is there really a difference?"

"I don't want you to regret anything." This, here, was why he'd called instead of landing on her doorstep uninvited.

She laughed. "You mean the way I threw myself at you this summer, and you pretended to have to babysit?"

"I did it for you."

"Oh, how very noble."

God, he wanted her. So, so bad. "So ask me again."

"Ask you what?"

"Ask me to come over."

"Aren't you the one who called me, asking if I was alone?"

"Ask me, Cat. If you still want it, ask me."

Another laugh from her, and then her voice was low, a kittenish purr. "Come over?"

Charles left the phone dangling against the booth.

Charles' lips burned against the inside of her thighs. Every soft moan coming from her beautiful mouth tested his iron resistance.

His tongue entered her. He wanted to be gentle, to tease the orgasm from her until she was begging him for it, but the shock of how wet she was... how delicious her nectar tasted... propelled him to bring her higher, higher, and higher, until she shuddered so hard her thighs almost snapped his neck.

She sounded so surprised as she came, and he knew he'd been right all along, that no man had never brought her to this point before. He slipped a finger inside her, to feel the intensity, and was not disappointed.

Charles looked down at Catherine, nude, legs spread but relaxed against the fabric of the couch, cheeks flushed. She gave him a lazy smile that somehow, at the same time, made his dick and his heart throb.

She snaked her hand forward and grasped him, and he grew harder in her touch. "I want it dirty," she whispered. Her tongue flitted across her lips. "The first time. The second time, I want to look at you."

A strange flutter passed through him. His breath was heavy, ragged, but he didn't hesitate. His hands gripped her hips and flipped her over, taking her surprised gasp as an encouragement.

His thumbs parted her from behind. Ah, how he wanted to eat more of her, to taste her desire, but if he didn't come soon, he would pass out. When he drove into her, she screamed in ecstasy and turned her head to look at him, biting her lips, eyes wild.

He filled her in seconds, and if she were anyone else, he'd be overcome with shame, but this was Catherine, and all he could think about was what came next, of looking into her eyes and seeing through to what was behind them when he spilled more of himself into her.

She turned, her breasts heaving with her gasping breath. "This means something to you," she said, sweet, husky, exhausted.

"You mean something to me," he said and entered her once more. He moved slowly, no longer shackled by his need to release. Her eyes closed for only a second before she left them open with a dreamy but intense look.

Her fingers pressed against the flesh of his bottom as she guided him in, out, slowly, perfectly. "We understand each other, don't we?"

Charles nodded. His eyes rolled back, but he forced himself to focus. On her. On her beautiful, welcoming, loving face. On seeing her, as she saw him.

Catherine lowered his face to her breast and he took it in his mouth, tenderly, as she caressed his face with both her hands, moaning with every current of their lovemaking.

He didn't leave her apartment for two days.

CHAPTER 13

The Mighty Steed

Augustus argued with a contractor in the other room. They'd told him they were behind on sub-contracting the painting of the walls, which they assured him had to be done before the flooring and furniture could be brought in.

His staff was only eleven—twelve, if you counted Evangeline, but she didn't think she counted when she was adamant about not taking a paycheck—but they were eager to move in and begin work assembling Volume One of Deschanel Magazine. It was supposed to be out in two weeks, but with the office buildout over six weeks behind, that date was unlikely.

Augustus was furious. She'd noted, as she began to know her brother better, that where he was easygoing about many things, he was quite exacting about others. Not everything in his life had, or deserved, a set standard, but when it did, he didn't respond well to disappointment.

Evangeline made the mistake of asking him why he didn't just let the staff writers do their work from home and have the editor come in and just work through the mess. Being flexible was key to the success of any big initiative. This was backed by science. Instead of thanking her for the helpful suggestion, he'd glared at her as if she'd grown a second, and then a third, head.

He'd been more short with her as of late, and she thought this might be because she'd been spending so much more time at the office. After that terrible end to her summer and that... that thing that had happened, that she could never, ever talk about, or think about, she'd thrown herself into whatever odd task Augustus had for her. She didn't even grumble about cleaning toilets anymore. Anything was better than having time to think.

His cheeks were flushed when he entered the breakroom. She was stacking cups in the cupboard, for the eventual employees upon their eventual arrival.

"What did he say?"

"Nothing but excuses," Augustus grumbled and stomped over to the sink. He took the glass she had in her hand and turned the faucet, filling it with water. "At least the damn water is on."

"When are the painters coming in?"

"Next fall at this rate." He emptied the glass in one sip and set it down. He leaned into the counter with both hands. "The hurricane was almost two months ago, and there was hardly any lasting damage. How is that a reason for a delay? And how are we no longer at the top of the list?"

Evangeline didn't tell him that repainting schools so children could return was probably a reasonable excuse. "We'll get Volume One out soon. Don't sweat it so much."

Augustus looked up. "Why aren't you in school?"

Evangeline was taken aback. "I haven't registered for classes. You know that. I'm taking time off."

"You already took a year off."

She shrugged. She hoped it looked nonchalant, for she certainly didn't feel that way. "I guess I'm taking two."

He sighed. "Evie..."

"You don't want me around? Is that it?"

Augustus shook his head. "No, that's not it at all. But the smartest one in the family shouldn't be wasting her time cleaning sinks and carrying out garbage."

"I don't mind it."

"That's not the point."

She didn't want to have this discussion. She had no words for him, no explanation or rational way of articulating the paralysis shackling her from moving forward. How even the thought of doing something unusual and different sent her heartrate soaring so high the sensation left her dizzy and reeling.

And there was no way in the world she would ever tell him what happened to her. She wouldn't do that to him. He might not survive this time.

"Okay," he said, leaning back, in a more welcoming stance. "Tell me, if you could go to school anywhere in the world, no limitations, where would you go?"

"Massachusetts Institute of Technology," Evangeline said with no hesitation.

Augustus laughed. "That was easy. Have you applied?"

Evangeline shook her head.

"Any reason why not?"

"I told you, I'm taking—"

"Another year off. Right." Augustus wiped his hands over the shadow of stubble that appeared overnight, aging him. He was a man now, in so many ways, and she remembered chasing him around the yard; how he'd humored her by being her mighty steed as she, Joan of Arc, Savior of France, rode in to face the evil English, north of Orléans.

"Besides, Mama would freak."

"Would she?" Augustus asked. "Colleen sent off to colleges across the country for med school. One in Scotland, too."

"Scotland?" Evangeline's head shot up. Was this true? She hated that Augustus knew this—Augustus, who was always the *last* to know—and she hadn't heard even a whisper.

"Mama thinks it would be good for her, too."

"How do you know?"

"Colleen told me," he said. "When I found her mail."

Evangeline relaxed a little. Of course Colleen would have to explain herself if Augustus learned her secret. "Bully for her, I guess."

"So, MIT."

She shrugged. "Just a thought. I'd be happy here, too."

Augustus glanced at the clock. "I'm leaving early tonight. You have a ride home? Want to take my car?"

"Leaving early? You?" She laughed. "Why?"

His eyes cast to the side. "It's nothing. I'm meeting Carolina for dinner. But it's nothing. She asked and I couldn't keep saying no."

Evangeline's grin spread. "You could say no. You've been saying no."

"You know how she is."

"You like her!"

Augustus flushed scarlet. "I didn't say that. She's nice, and I don't want to keep hurting her feelings."

"So you're gonna string her along and break her heart later? Or is your plan to marry her to avoid all that?"

Augustus rolled his eyes. "I don't have to explain myself to you. Do you need my car, or do you have other plans?"

"I don't have other plans," Evangeline said quickly. "If I take your car, how will you get home?" Her mouth dropped open. "Aggie!"

"Get your mind out of the gutter," he hissed. "Charles is coming home tonight. I phoned him earlier and he said to swing by Cat's if one of us needed a ride back to Vacherie."

"Cat? Who's Cat?"

"His girlfriend," Augustus said. He cleared his throat. "Secret girlfriend. No one's supposed to know."

"Why would Charles suddenly care what anyone thinks? Is she hideous?"

"Quite the opposite." Augustus draped his sport coat over his arm. "But she happens to be Colin Sullivan's ex."

Evangeline gaped in amazement. *That* Catherine. That took balls, even for Charles. "Say no more. Where are your keys?"

Augustus dug them from his pocket and lobbed them across the room at her. She caught them with ease and dangled the key from her finger. "Not even a mile over the speed limit, Evie."

The 1963 Aston Martin DB5 had been a gift from his mother when he graduated high school, and though he was not prone to the indulgence one would normally possess in driving such a car, because it was his he treated it with meticulous attention.

"Speedometers are imperfect technology," Evangeline said, grinning as his scowl deepened. "But I'll obey insofar as I'm not accountable for any shortcomings your car had before I slipped behind the wheel."

He groaned under his breath and nodded as he left the room.

Was he downplaying this thing with Carolina? Evangeline cursed herself for being so jealous. If anyone deserved happiness, it was Augustus.

But there was already Charles and Cat; Colleen and Rory; Elizabeth and Connor; Maureen and her misery.

Evangeline was twisted and broken. Objectively speaking, she was not as beautiful as her sisters. Not as interesting as Charles. Not as intriguing as Augustus. She was a genius, but in societal terms, this made her a freak, not something to be desired. Though she knew better, deep down, she woke up in the middle of the night certain the whole world could see what had happened to her, and the taint it left upon her, leaving her marked as defective. A stink that would invite predators and turn away suitors.

The quiet buzz of the electricity, and nothing else, sent a chill through her. She rushed out of the office, her brother's keys promising at least one healthy thrill on the return to her anguish.

HOMESCHOOLING WAS THE BEST.

Elizabeth had never minded the school part of going to school every day. She liked learning, though she didn't know how much, how curious her mind actually was, until it was free to be so. The world was so big! So much to explore! And out here, in their isolated old plantation house in the country, the shackles of a tortured world didn't exist.

There was something about the family home… about the house in particular… that muted her visions. Always had, ever since she was a toddler. She didn't know what it was, and she didn't care.

It felt so good not to care.

She wasn't completely free of premonitions here, but they were vague and indistinct, like a television out of tune. Whenever Charles was around, she was filled with acute foreboding, but nothing specific ever jumped out of her. She saw anguish, but never death. Never the final act.

Charles was the first one to notice the difference in her.

"You've got a twinkle in your eyes, Lizzy Lou," he said one day, after he'd come home from seeing his girlfriend. That she *had* seen, and she'd seen how it ended, too. "The country looks good on you."

"Might look good on you too if you were ever around," she accused, teasing.

"You've been spending a lot of time with that little Sullivan squirt. Anything I should know about that?"

"As I said…"

"Do you need me?" His smile ebbed. "Do you?"

No, but you'll be married soon, and then I'll see you even less. You're the only one who's ever looked at me and seen more than a freak to be pitied. "You wish!" she challenged, and he chased her up the stairs and into her room for some tickles, which she was very nearly too old for, but these moments were never forever.

Connor was allowed over on the weekends, although allowed was a generous word. Connor's mother, Savannah, treated weekends like getaways from her children, and with dramatic flourish. She'd seen the opportunity for what it was, and began sending *both* her sons over every Friday after classes were over.

Connor's twin brother, Thomas, was all right, but he was in a completely different league. Where Connor was shy and curious, and a touch funny, Thomas wanted to build things just to knock them down. His personality eclipsed everyone around him, not the least of which was Connor himself.

But Elizabeth and Connor, through clever planning, found a better place for the precocious Thomas: Maureen's clubhouse. The small building was an old storage shed from the days Ophélie was a working plantation. Charles had taken pity on her and spent one summer day cleaning it out, and even gave it a fresh coat of paint. Elizabeth didn't have the heart to tell him Maureen wasn't going in there to play dolls.

Elizabeth didn't want to know what Maureen was doing with the almost-thirteen-year-old Thomas, and she didn't care, either. No one ever wondered how their choices affected her, when that's all she could ever think about, her whole life.

Connor lay at the end of her bed looking as if the image coming to life on her Lite Brite was the next Picasso.

"Wanna go down to the river?" she asked.

He groaned in disgust. "It's way too hot to play outside. Ask me again at Halloween."

She returned the groan. It wasn't so much that she wanted to play outside. She never did. But the big house had ghosts, past and present, and she never felt them as acutely as she did when she was home alone. Aside from Maureen and Thomas doing god-knows-what in her clubhouse, across the property, Elizabeth and Connor had all of Ophélie to themselves.

It wasn't only the ghosts. She had never divined her own future, not once, and she didn't know if that was a defect or the intended outcome of her gift, but she had a powerful fear that being alone, where she was unaffected by the anguish of others, was when she was most likely to find this element of her soothsaying come to life.

Connor sounded his victory cry and raised the Lite Brite above his head. "At last!"

Elizabeth resisted the urge to tell him it took her less than five minutes to do her templates and gave him a diplomatic, if condescending, grin instead. "Let's see."

He rolled back to his stomach and stretched it out to her with one arm.

Elizabeth frowned. "What is this?"

"Stop pretending. I know you can see it."

"Ah, yes. A wizard whose robe was stolen by this strange snail in the corner."

"It's a damn snowman, and that's a tree," he barked and snatched it back. "Which I *know* you *know* because this stupid thing only has about ten different templates to choose from you and you've already done them all a thousand times."

Elizabeth beamed. "You're right. But there's sixteen. And I've done them all a million times."

"That's not possible."

"Did you do the math?"

"No, but it's not possible."

"Do the math and prove me wrong."

She'd thought this would call his bluff, but he surprised her by digging in his bookbag for a pencil and paper. Amused, she watched him tick the numbers off in his fingers as he came to the slow realization the math he was trying to do was more than he'd bargained for.

"Didn't bring a calculator?" she taunted as his brow furrowed into a series of tight wrinkles.

His pencil scribbled away. "Who can afford one of those?"

Elizabeth had one in her desk drawer, but wouldn't say so. Not because she was ashamed to be from a family who could afford one for their children—his could, too, they were just more miserly about where their money went—but because she wanted the pleasure of seeing him suffer through his pride.

Connor was on her bed sorting through his math quandary in one moment, and then in the next *he stood before a tomb in a cemetery, a man grown. Both hands folded across his torso, across the neat suit he'd worn for the first time burying his child, and was now wearing for the second time burying his wife.*

Elizabeth gasped and fell back against the wall.

Connor was alert in an instant. He threw the toy to the side, forgotten, and scrambled over the blankets toward her. "Lizzy, talk to me."

Rain fell, blanketing the cemetery and the shallow, muddy ground. Connor tried to reach for the hand of the one next to him, but the figure slipped farther away. He could not believe he was here. It wasn't real. That had to be it… God would not first take his only daughter, and then his beloved wife. Life was not so cruel. God was not so cruel.

The room snapped to and fro as Connor shook her. "Lizzy, breathe, talk to me."

The cemetery dissolved into the future, where it belonged. She'd tried, tried to see the names on the tomb, to understand what it was she was seeing, but the visions never worked that way. She tried, and tried, but they only showed what they chose her to see.

"It was you," she said, gathering herself back into the present. She focused on breathing and on grounding herself to the room, to the bed, to the house.

"Me?" Connor's grip on her lessened. "You saw my future?"

Elizabeth nodded. Her mouth hung half-open, pairing neatly with her blank stare.

"Well, that's new, right? You've never seen my future before." She couldn't tell if he was fearful or curious, or both.

"No," she said. "And don't ask me to tell you what I saw."

Connor fell back into a pile of blankets. "You promised me you would if you ever saw me in your visions."

"I never promised that." Or had she? She couldn't have known it would be so dark… so devoid of hope. Not for her sweet Connor, full of life.

"You did, Elizabeth."

"Using my full name doesn't make your point better."

"You did promise," he insisted. He wasn't smiling. "You promised no secrets, and this is a secret."

"You don't want to know."

"Knowing I don't want to know makes me want to know even more!"

She sighed. The last of the cemetery left her. "I should have lied and said it was about Maureen."

"Why would you say that?"

"One day, you'll regret knowing me," Elizabeth said. She turned away when the tears burned her eyes.

"Nothing you've ever told me has made me regret knowing you, and I promised nothing ever would."

"Yeah, well, we're kids."

"Kids who know how important a promise is." He reached forward and touched his soft hand to hers. When she gave a weird look, he withdrew it. "If you don't tell me, you're the one who doesn't trust me."

"It's fuzzy," she said after a pause. "What I saw is just the bad stuff, but not enough of the details to help you."

Connor shrugged. "Pretend you're telling me about someone else, then."

"But I'm not."

"Lizzy."

"Swear to me."

"What? Anything."

"That you won't hate me when I tell you. It's not my fault... I just see it... I can't..."

"I *know*," he said. "I know how it works. I promise."

She turned her palms up. "You... have a family in the future."

Connor smiled. "That's not so bad."

She inhaled hard. "Except some of them die. I don't... I don't know how. A daughter, and then your wife. That's all I know."

Connor's expression withdrew from one of interest to one she could no longer read. "Wow. That sucks."

Elizabeth nodded. Tears raced down her cheeks. He'd leave her now, and she'd never see him again, her only friend.

He chucked her on the arm and then grinned. "No big deal, right? I just won't get married! The bachelor life sounds way more appealing anyway."

"But you will marry," Elizabeth said quietly. "And she will die."

CHAPTER 14

Nights in White Satin

Colleen didn't have the heart to wake Rory. His mouth fell wide against the pillow, and he was so far lost to his dreams that he didn't make a single sound. His mother, Josephine, had just recovered from surgery to remove a malignant tumor in her chest, and he'd spent every hour of his days at her bedside, comforting his father and siblings, retreating to Colleen's bed in the evening for his own comfort.

She'd told herself in the beginning that she let him in each night out of something resembling pity, but she knew better. Despite what Ophelia had tried to tell her, and despite her own instincts that told her that her future was elsewhere, Colleen couldn't cut the last and final cord needed to move on.

As he fell asleep in her arms last night, she didn't know if she ever could.

Colleen heard whispering from Charles' room. She paused outside his door. He was bold, bringing Catherine here, when Rory slept two rooms away. She'd kept her brother's secret, because it wasn't hers to share, but his carelessness would catch up if he wasn't careful.

Irish Colleen caught her on her way out the door.

"Augustus told me you're going to see Ophelia, the two of you," her mother said. She tied her apron about her waist. Soon, the smells of breakfast would waft through the old floorboards and wake the upstairs.

"He's going to meet me there. She's home today," Colleen responded. She tensed, dubious of her mother's intentions. There had never been love lost between Irish Colleen and Ophelia, and though Colleen wasn't supposed to know, this all came to a head when Irish Colleen approached the old woman in search of a more supernatural solution to Maureen's predicament. Ophelia had said no, and then some.

"A longer stay than they anticipated, yes?"

Colleen nodded. She searched around for her purse, before realizing she'd left it in her room. She hoped she could retrieve it without waking Rory. "The pneumonia caused other complications, and she took longer to recover than they'd hoped."

Irish Colleen ran her hands over the old fabric of the apron, which had been her mother's, and one of the few things from her old life she'd brought into her marriage. Colleen knew nothing about the apron or her grandmother, only that the stains must tell a fascinating story. "The old woman and I are not on the best of terms. We never have been."

Colleen said nothing. Pointing out Irish Colleen's narrow-minded view of the family she married into wouldn't change the fact of it.

"But she's always been there for August and his children. And... she's been helpful to you as well, more, I suppose, than I have."

"That's not true, Mama," Colleen said quickly, though the words cut to the bone for all the truth of them. "Tante Ophelia has helped me learn more about who our family is, and that's important. But she's not my mother."

Irish Colleen nodded in an offhand way, as if it wasn't about her daughter's response at all. "I wish her well. That's all I mean to say."

"Thank you," Colleen said. She eyed the stairs, where she still needed to obtain her purse. "I'll tell her."

"Do that." She turned toward the kitchen and then looked

back. “Oh, can you pick up a pack of pencils for your sisters while you’re in town? I could run into Vacherie, but they charge twice as much and it makes my blood boil.”

“Of course. Anything else?”

Irish Colleen thought about it. “See if the cabbage looks healthy. The Piggly Wiggly won’t have their shipment of fresh vegetables until tomorrow. My vegetable garden seems to have been invaded by something from the devil after the cane harvest, and I wouldn’t feed it to my enemy.”

Colleen brightened. “Corned beef? What’s the occasion?”

“No occasion,” her mother said. “Though Charles has invited his girlfriend for supper, and this is a first.”

“Cat?” Colleen’s eyes nearly bugged out. “Tonight? For supper?”

Connor and Thomas were here… Rory might be here… had Charles lost his mind?

“Yes, Colleen, repeating the words doesn’t alter them in any way.”

She decided to stop worrying about her brother’s impending war with the Sullivans. Ophelia had given her the advice to stop focusing on things beyond her control, and while it went against everything in her nature, she found it liberating. To think she could just walk away from a problem!

“Don’t forget the pencils. Their last ones are down to nubs.”

“How is homeschooling going?” Colleen asked.

“Oh, it’s coming along, by the by. Elizabeth is thriving. Maureen just needs some time to get used to it,” Irish Colleen replied. She reached into her apron to retrieve the duster and focused on a spot missed earlier. “Not that it’s your concern, Colleen. I can see that mind of yours spinning already.”

Colleen put her hands up in surrender. “I was only asking, Mama.”

“No, you were searching for an opportunity, and you won’t find any here.”

. . .

Charles traced his tongue over Cat's lower lip. It glistened with his come, and the saltiness was unwelcome but the soft, guttural moan passing through her mouth to his certainly was.

Her kitten heels brushed the side of his ear as he shoved his weight against the back of her thighs. God, how he loved it when she wore nothing but these red patent heels. These, only these, the ones he'd bought her, that she'd at first blushed at, and then left on for their sex games, because she knew.

They never spoke of Colin. She didn't have to say that the sex with Colin had been boring for him to know, for every new thing he tried on her—things he'd never tried with anyone, when he thought he'd done everything—sent her over the edge in mingled shock and titillation. He loved to keep her guessing. To go right when she expected left. To blow her mind, which blew his.

Charles loved her, but they never spoke of that, either.

But he knew more about Catherine Connelly than he knew about his own sisters. She wanted to travel the world and write books and poems about her experiences. Her eyes lit up when she talked about standing at the base of the Eiffel Tower, or peering through the crackled and crumbling walls of the Colosseum at a past she could hardly begin to understand. That she would never do these things broke his heart. She was too practical. The need to please her family and achieve the goals they'd set out for her was too great.

"I'll send you around the world," he promised. "Ten times over."

"How dizzy I'd be!"

Dizzy. Charles was dizzy, and for once, this sensation didn't involve drugs. In fact, he hadn't touched blow in over a month, and he'd even cut back on smoking and drinking. *Cat* was a drug, and even when he was too tired to find his clothes, he wanted her. How he wanted her. All the time. Always.

How had he never known this?

"Why aren't you inside me?" she purred.

All the blood sailed straight from Charles' head. But his

stomach screamed at him, a reminder he'd skipped both lunch and dinner the day before. "Let's eat and then I'll never leave."

She laughed and gave him a playful push. "I feel your priorities, Deschanel."

"You're gonna be feeling something—"

"Breakfast!" Irish Colleen's voice boomed through the hallway. Charles waited until her footsteps disappeared back down the stairs, and then nibbled on Cat's nipple.

"Hey!" she cried and pressed the stiletto of her heel into his bare chest. "If I have to wait, so do you."

"I said I was hungry. I never said what I was gonna eat..."

"Charles August Deschanel." She threw his shirt at him. It landed on his head.

"You do have your loafers, right?"

Catherine looked offended. "As if you really think I'd wear these heels in front of your mother."

He shrugged. "You did tell me you wanted to make an impression."

"A *good* impression," she chided, and then the illusion was over. The heels lay in a discarded pile in the corner, for later. She slipped her sundress over her narrow frame. The fabric brushed across her breasts, which gave a light bounce at the resistance. No bra. His stomach quivered.

Cat ran her fingers through her hair in a frenzy before his mirror. She stopped. "Charles, do you really think this is a good idea? Truly?"

"You don't want to eat with my family?"

Her hands dropped to her sides. "You know that's not true."

They both traded places, back and forth, on the efficacy of telling their families and bringing their relationship out in the open. Some days, Charles was convinced the world should know, and that it would all work out. Others, he despaired to the point of making himself physically sick.

Was gaining Cat worth more than losing Colin?

Some days, he thought he knew the answer. But how could he think straight, when she looked at him the way she always did?

They couldn't go on like this, either, though. Loving her was exquisite torture. It was having what you wanted, while knowing it was never really yours. And he had never wanted anything more.

Catherine opened the door and winked. "Let's go eat so you can refuel, old man."

"You'll pay for that."

"I sure hope so."

As Charles hopped into his pants and buckled them, he heard an exclamation from the hallway. Catherine gasped.

He shuffled out, and there was Rory.

His mouth flapped through a series of attempted starts.

"Rory..." Catherine started. She took a step and stopped. "I didn't know you were here."

"That's what you have to say?" He was aghast. "You didn't know I was here?"

"You can't tell him."

"Can't tell who?"

"You know who."

Rory moved toward them. "Say his name, Cat."

"Back off, Sullivan," Charles warned. "This isn't your business. Don't make me make it your business."

"That doesn't even make sense, Charles." He shook his head. "Cat, I didn't ask to be put in the middle of this. You did that. But he's my *brother*. I can't lie to him."

"It's not lying to just say nothing," she said. Her voice cracked.

"Why are you so hot about this anyway?" Charles barked. "They broke up months ago. I know Colin won't be too stoked, but he can't expect her to stay single forever."

Rory laughed. He ignored Charles and looked directly at Cat. "He doesn't know, does he?"

"Know *what*?" Charles asked. The shithead needed to stop, and now. He didn't want to have to pulverize Colleen's boyfriend. She'd never let him hear the end of it.

Catherine burst into tears. She buried her face in her palms.

Rory said nothing. He waited, and in the silence, Charles deduced what they knew and he did not.

She'd been seeing them both.

"It's not what you think," Catherine sobbed. "Colin needed someone when Josephine got sick, and he didn't have anyone else..."

"He had me!" Charles boomed. He backed away from them both, until he smacked into the wall. "He had Rory, and Patrick, and Chelsea!"

"He was so sad, Charles... you don't know how hard it was to see him like that... I don't love him like that, anymore, but I didn't know how to say no."

"Should probably tell Colin that," Rory snapped. "News to him."

Catherine turned her back to Rory and implored Charles with those eyes of hers, those beautiful, searching eyes he'd murder for. Wouldn't be the first time. "I should have told you. I wish I'd told you. But, Charles, what I feel for you..."

He wanted to shove her, shove her so hard she bounced off the wall and fell into a heap at his feet, reduced to begging. His breathing raged out of control, and he thought for a moment he was actually crying.

"You can't even say it," Charles said. "Because it was just fun for you."

Her head shook so hard her face was a blur. "No, it wasn't just fun. It's *not* just fun, Charles. It's... it's..." She choked on her sobs and curled her lips inward.

"Jesus Christ, Cat. I'm going home. You either break this off, or you tell Colin, or I will." Rory pushed past them and ran down the stairs.

"Go," Charles said. "Maybe he'll drive you home, if you ask real nice."

Cat reached for his face, and he broke away. "Charles—"

You broke my heart. You ripped it from my chest, when until you I didn't even know I fucking had one. You set it on fire, and now there's a hole in my chest where all the good stuff died.

Charles disappeared back into his room and locked the door. When she beat her fists against the wood, he flipped on the radio and sent the dial to max.

With closed eyes, he rifled through the drawer. He didn't need to see. He knew where it was.

He pressed the tiny spoon to his nose and inhaled, once, twice, three, then four times, until he was dizzy once more, but with something safer, safer.

COLLEEN WAITED UNTIL THE INTENSE CONFRONTATION at the top of the stairs had come to a dramatic conclusion. Rory said only that he'd call her later as he blew past her without so much as a proper goodbye. So much for not waking him.

She found Catherine outside Charles' room, beating her fists weakly at the wood as her knees buckled.

"You should go," Colleen said, as gently as she could manage. "When he's made up his mind about something, he needs time."

"I'm in love with him," Cat whispered. Her hands fell back from the door, and she looked surprised at her own words. "I love him. I love Charles."

Colleen sighed. She touched Cat's arm and guided her away from Charles' door. "Okay, maybe tell him later, when he's not so angry, all right?"

"He should know," Cat said, faraway, tired, dreamy. "He needs to know."

It won't matter a whit. Charles isn't capable of what you want from him. And he'll be married off to someone he didn't choose, and there's nothing he or anyone can do about it. "And you should. When you both have had some time to cool off."

"Yeah," Cat said. "Okay. Sure. You're right."

Colleen knew she shouldn't let the poor girl wander off in this state. With another sigh, this one more controlled, she said, "I'll drive you into New Orleans. I'm headed there anyway. I'll meet you out front."

"Thanks, Colleen."

Colleen went to grab her purse. On the way back out, Evangeline flew by in tears, past the room, and to the end of the hall, where their shared bathroom was.

Colleen paused for a moment, and then left.

CHAPTER 15
Peace is at Hand

Augustus had never tried his powers of persuasion by phone. Even now, he didn't entirely understand the conditions required to make it work. When he'd resolved to use them on someone, he went through a sort of physical change; straightening his shoulders, assuming a veil of authority. He focused his mind on sharing a belief, and the belief was shared.

The dean at MIT was a friendly, if somewhat humorless, man. With great surprise, Augustus learned the man already knew who Evangeline was, and, in fact, had her college transcript in a file for prospects.

"I must say, I was disappointed when we didn't receive an application from Evangeline. I can't imagine a better school for a student of her caliber."

Augustus adjusted the phone. "Forgive me, I don't understand."

"The top schools in the major metropolitan areas send us their most promising candidates each year. Think of it the way college sports recruiters scout high schools for prospects, except we aren't out in the field, and we don't pay for talent."

"If you went to all that trouble, why just put her in a folder?"

The man coughed. "We aren't in the business of soliciting

students, Mr. Deschanel. As you may well imagine, we receive far more submissions each year than we know what to do with. Having the top minds already identified helps us ensure that none of them get lost in the system."

"I see," Augustus said. It seemed he wouldn't get the chance to test his skills by phone, after all.

"May I ask, where has your sister been attending college, if not here?"

"She hasn't," Augustus replied gruffly, and this, he thought, was where it all unraveled.

"Oh. Well then."

"It's not for lack of motivation," Augustus explained. "Evangeline has been helping me start my business, Deschanel Media Group. She's learning many practical aspects of business, which are invaluable to anyone. I couldn't have done it without her."

"Yes, yes, of course. That's splendid. Work ethic is, sadly, the one thing we cannot teach our students."

"What would it take to get my sister enrolled for winter term?"

Papers shuffled on the other end of the phone, across the country. "Well, you see, winter term is for existing students only. All new students to MIT come through our orientation week in the fall term, which has a number of events assigned to help them feel at home. As a second year student, of course, she could choose to skip her fall term, though I don't know why anyone would." He covered the phone with his hand, and what he said next was unintelligible. "Ah, yes, my secretary has kindly reminded me that we now do orientation in spring as well."

"Spring term, then."

"We would be honored to have her here, of course," said the dean. "It would only be a formality, but I do need her application on file, for accounting and auditing purposes. "Are you using a facsimile machine yet?"

Augustus had considered the investment, but saw no use in owning a system most of the world couldn't afford to use. "I'll have my assistant send the application by mail, the fastest speed available."

"Wonderful. You can let your assistant know that both Tulane and Loyola have copies of our application. Will she be needing financial aid?" The dean must have realized his error, for he chuckled. "Forgive me, I know she won't."

"You'll have it on your desk by the end of week."

"Very good. And Mr. Deschanel?"

"Yes?"

"Please, there's no need to send the application fee. The paperwork is for our records only. Evangeline may consider herself an MIT student this spring."

"Pleasure talking to you."

Augustus cradled the phone. The large, open office space was empty now, but hours earlier had been abuzz with activity. Their first edition of Deschanel Magazine was nearly ready, and his adman, James, had secured support from some of the leaders in New Orleans business. Restaurants and hotels had already ordered their copies, and he'd even gotten calls from Baton Rouge asking after availability.

He should be happy. He understood, at the surface, all was well in his life. His goals were coming to life right before his eyes. He was on the precipice of something great, beyond his imagination.

Where there should be joy, there was only hollow acceptance.

The reasons were no mystery. And while what Augustus told the dean was true, that he couldn't have done any of this without Evangeline, he was now somewhat of a reluctant expert on the topic of a drowning loved one. She was drowning here, and he wouldn't lose her, too.

Augustus hadn't yet hired an assistant, so he grabbed his coat and briefcase and went to go see about the application.

Carolina had been hanging around again. She came and went like the wind, and Colleen couldn't decide if she was just late to the realization they'd grown apart, or knew and didn't care.

To make matters weirder, Carolina knew Colleen and Rory were in an "on again" phase of their relationship saga, and, worse, knew she was second fiddle, the one Rory ran to when Colleen turned him away.

Carolina's constant checking of doors, no matter what room they were in, eventually gave her away.

"Car… you're going to get your heart broken, you know."

"What're you talking about, Colleen?" She rifled through the box of records she'd brought over. Colleen had noted Carolina flocked to music as therapy the same way Colleen retreated into studying. The more anxious her friend was, the more she changed the record, the artist, the volume, the song. "I told you, I was only having fun with Rory. He loves you. I'm cool. I dig it."

"You know I don't mean Rory."

Carolina flashed her doe eyes, which might work on others, but had never worked on Colleen. She tried to push her annoyance down. Carolina might be playing at something, but there was no maliciousness in her. No guile. "What? Oh, Augustus?" She waved her hand, which held a Supremes record. "We're just talking. It's nothing."

"He's not like other men, Carolina."

"You think he's into boys or something?"

"No, I don't think he's into boys."

Carolina flung her blond hair over one shoulder. She checked the door again, likely without realizing it. "You don't have to protect your brother from little old me."

"It's not Augustus I'm trying to protect," Colleen said.

Augustus parked his car at the gap in the levee, a mile from Ophélie.

On the passenger seat lay the newspaper he'd picked up at the office after he'd finished running his errands to get Evangeline's paperwork completed and sent to the appropriate place.

PEACE IS AT HAND, the headline read. *Top foreign policy strategist, Henry Kissinger, following a visit to South Vietnam, has announced the administration is one session away from ending the war.*

He looked again to his right. Madeline sat in the seat, picking at the shreds of denim fraying around her thighs.

"When will you be okay?" he asked her.

"I'll never be okay," she said. She licked her fingers and ran them over the fractured denim, smoothing out the damage. "But the war ending would give me some peace. I just hope I'm alive to see it."

Augustus laid his head on the hard leather steering wheel and sobbed.

COLLEEN WAS A LIGHT SLEEPER, SO LIGHT NOTHING MORE than a gust of wind could rouse her. So she heard the door downstairs open and close, and through deduction, reasoned it must be Augustus.

She was also awake to acknowledge Carolina carefully setting her blanket aside and slipping out of the room.

This is another example of something outside your control. Let it go. Let others make their mistakes. They are theirs to make, not yours to fix.

Colleen closed her eyes and tried to sleep, but she wouldn't get much. Staying out of it was one thing; being rid of her worry was another.

AUGUSTUS LAY ON THE TOP OF HIS BED. HE DIDN'T bother with his clothes, or the covers, though his mother had turned them back, as she had since he was a boy.

He wasn't a boy anymore, though. Nothing about him felt like that person anymore, and it wasn't any one thing, but a culmination of events and losses, working together to reshape him.

He didn't belong in this world, but he didn't know how to leave it behind.

Augustus didn't look up when his door opened. With luck, they'd see his closed eyes for the lack of invitation they conveyed.

The door closed again. He opened his eyes, but the visitor wasn't gone.

Carolina looped her hands behind her back and regarded him with a soft, curious look.

"I need to get some sleep," he said. He truly didn't want to hurt her, but it seemed inevitable, past the point where that was still possible.

"But you're not," she said. "I can't sleep either."

"I'll fall asleep. I always do."

She sat in the middle of his bed, and her back brushed his torso where he lay. The back of her hand fell against his cheek, and she brushed it gently. Her finger passed over the corner of his eyes, still damp. "I don't have anywhere for the hurt to go either."

"Carolina..."

"Everyone thinks I'm the fun, bubbly friend who always wants to have a good time. They don't think there's much else to me," she went on. She brought her hand back and wound it in with her other one. She wrung them in her lap. "Not even Colleen realizes I do that because I don't want anyone to know how dark I feel inside."

Augustus pulled himself up. He didn't know how to respond, but he was listening.

"When Daniel died, the whole community came together for my parents. I don't think my mom made dinner for at least half a year, we had so many casserole dishes. I didn't realize you could put so many damn things *in* a casserole." Carolina looked at her hands. "They tried to be there for me, but they were broken, too. I didn't want them to hurt more by seeing me hurting. And by the time they pulled their lives back to something normal, I'd never learned to process my grief, but I'd learned how to hide it."

"How long ago did this happen?"

"The summer between my sophomore and junior years. All my friends were on vacations with their families. Colleen was at summer camp. I spent all day and night in my bedroom, and when school was back, I'd figured out how to answer people's questions without breaking down."

"How?" Augustus asked.

Half her mouth curved in a smile. "I changed the subject to something more fun. No one really wants to talk about a dead kid, anyway. The novelty wears off quick, and your friends move on, so you have to do the same."

Augustus' hand moved across the blanket. It tickled the side of hers. "I'm sorry you felt so alone." He thought of Madeline; how he'd never understood her, not really, but had sensed how deeply she needed someone to understand her and be her protector, so she could protect others.

"I see you doing it, too." Carolina turned to look at him. "Your magazine. Sleeping at the office. You don't want anyone to see you moping, because you don't want them to worry, but you also don't want to go *there*. You can't win." She slid her fingers over his. "I know you think I'm a silly girl, with not much to offer. I'm not blind. I know you don't really wanna see me, Augustus, but that's why I keep coming around, you know? Because I wish someone had seen how alone I was and hadn't ignored me when I said I was fine."

Augustus leaned forward and kissed her. Her lips were soft and warm, and after the initial shock, she fell into the kiss. He'd never done it before and wondered if what he was doing was right, or if she would think he was a fool with no technique.

"I'm sorry," he said, but her arms were wrapped around his neck and they fell back diagonally across his neatly made bed, where no one but he had slept since he was a baby.

Carolina maneuvered her body atop his. She peppered his cheeks, his chin, his forehead with kisses, moving her lips across his skin like silk passing over.

Augustus didn't know what was happening. He didn't have

time to make sense of it, or the experience to evaluate where this was leading. He knew only that he didn't want this, but also that he did, so very, very badly. He was sick with how terribly he craved the touch of another, and to know the love everyone around him, except him, had known.

Carolina's hands went to work on the buttons of his shirt. His arms hung at his sides and he had to do something, so he ran them across the soft cotton of her sweater. When they found flesh, he moved her sweater up and over her head. She helped him free herself of the fabric and tossed it away, somewhere.

She bucked backward. Her arms strained behind her back, and then her bra, too, fell away.

Augustus stared at her. He'd never seen a woman nude before, not even in a magazine. He wasn't interested in such things; felt they cheapened what was real. Carolina. She really was so beautiful. He didn't deserve her affections, or her concern, but she was here, and tonight, she was his.

They rolled around in an awkward attempt to rid themselves of their pants, tangling in the moment, in the kisses, in the heat between them. When there was nothing left to separate their flesh, Augustus knew this next move was his, but he was terrified of disappointing her after all she'd done for him.

Carolina tugged at him, and he maneuvered until he was looking down at her this time. Her soft, milky breasts, her golden hair. He'd never given very much thought to what this first time would be like, but not even in his fleeting considerations had he imagined how hard his heart would beat, and how much he'd feel for someone he hardly knew.

Her hand reached between his legs. Augustus gasped. She'd sensed, as she sensed so much else, his fears and gently addressed them. Perhaps it was her encouragement, or perhaps years of animal instinct bred into every last organic creature, but Augustus found his way inside her and the world erupted into controlled chaos.

Everything fell away. His pain. His fear. His self-control.

"Just be," Carolina said as he moved within her; as she ran her fingers over his flesh, claiming him.

Augustus woke before the sun had crested over the east lands.

Carolina's face was nestled into his chest. Her long, silken hair fell over his bare chest in waves. She snored softly.

The halo around the night before had fallen away to reveal the reality that had kept him from such moments all his life.

He carefully untangled her and slipped back into the clothing he'd worn the day before. The sloppiness of this was close to horrifying, but he knew what he had to do, and if he didn't leave now... if she woke and looked at him again, as she had last night... he'd be lost.

Augustus looked at her one last time, and then let the door click softly behind him.

Colleen said nothing to Carolina when she snuck back in that morning. She almost reached for her friend when she heard the soft crying, pressed into the pillow but still obvious, but something hard in her heart prevented the gesture. If her friend didn't want her advice, then she didn't deserve her comfort.

Colleen's heart ached at the coldness, but she couldn't will herself to be a bigger person.

Carolina never explained where she'd been. When they were called down to breakfast, Carolina rolled out of bed with a heavy sigh, but came down as well.

The whole family was there. All except Augustus.

Carolina's eyes darted around looking for an explanation, but she said nothing.

"Wonderful, now that we're all here, I have some news to share," Irish Colleen said. Maureen and Elizabeth, hands linked for the usual Grace that started meals, dropped their hands and exchanged looks.

"Is someone hurt?" Evangeline asked, in a panic. "Dead?"

"The news isn't always bad around here, Evangeline," Irish Colleen chided. "You probably see Augustus isn't here this morning. That's because he's been busy, down at Sullivan & Associates attending to business."

"What business?" Colleen asked.

Irish Colleen folded and re-folded her napkin. "As you children know, it is within your right as a Deschanel, to claim a property when you become an adult. The heir's line gets first pick, and certain properties follow certain rules. None of you have done so yet, but you could, if you so choose. Charles will live here at Ophélie when he marries and has a family of his own. As the second son, Augustus has the right to claim Magnolia Grace, on Prytania, in the Garden District."

"That house is huge," Elizabeth said. She whistled. "Almost as big as The Gardens. Why would he want that?"

"It's his," Irish Colleen said with a light shrug. "And, this morning, Augustus signed the paperwork to make that official. The house is his. He's moving in today."

Carolina cried out. Her hands flew to her mouth to hide it.

"I don't understand. It's a Sunday. This couldn't have waited?" Colleen asked.

"It means Augustus is done here," Charles said. He reached for the breakfast rolls and popped one in his mouth, impatient. "He wants to be his own man. He can't do that here."

Carolina's cries tugged at Colleen's heart. She slipped her hand over her friend's.

"It's not you," she whispered. "It really isn't."

Elizabeth directed her words at the two of them. "Augustus is doing what he needs to do to step away from the past. This isn't because you had sex."

"Elizabeth!" Irish Colleen and Colleen exclaimed at the same time.

Carolina whimpered and fled from the table. Colleen hesitated for only a moment before she went after her.

"Car," she said. "It's not you."

"I wasn't trying to push him over the edge, Colleen," Carolina cried. "I wanted to bring him back from it."

"Maybe," Colleen said, "that's exactly what you did. Maybe you did save him."

Carolina wiped at her eyes. She breathed in and closed her eyes. "I'll never know, will I?" She grabbed her keys and disappeared out the front door.

Colleen wanted to follow, to give her more reassurances, but she couldn't bring herself to add deception to heartbreak. Carolina, Rory, Cat. They had all suffered so much in loving a Deschanel, when Deschanels did nothing but cause ruin and pain.

She knew then what she'd known for a long time, and what Ophelia had tried to tell her for months.

Colleen had to persuade Rory to move on and away from her. And maybe, just maybe, he'd find a way to love Carolina, and they could be happy. United in their experiences with a family incapable of anything real.

Elizabeth appeared in the foyer. "He'll be okay, Colleen."

"Yeah," Colleen said. "But for how long?"

Elizabeth's silence was the only answer.

WINTER 1970

VACHERIE, LOUISIANA
NEW ORLEANS, LOUISIANA

CHAPTER 16

She Needs Her Sister

Evangeline knew what was in the envelope before she opened it, but what she didn't know was why she'd received it.

The Massachusetts Institute of Technology is pleased to welcome you...

She let the letter fall to her desk. She had never so much as taken an application home. The guidance counselor at the high school knew she was interested, but the office workers were about as useful as a vacuum cleaner on the moon. Evangeline wasn't even sure the woman remembered her name, let alone any nuance about her desires for the future. She might be the smartest Deschanel, but she was far from the one everyone cared about.

Colleen knew, but Evangeline doubted her sister would bother. Even now, she dropped her eyes when they passed in the hall, except on the rare occasion she chose to berate her.

Colleen didn't know what she didn't know, and sometimes the temptation to spell it out for her was so, so tempting.

She'd only told one other about her dream of going to MIT...

Augustus.

Tell me, if you could go to school anywhere in the world, no limitations, where would you go?

Evangeline dug her hand around in the key jar for her set. Her birthday present had been the car she insisted she didn't need, but had already been so relieved to have.

She didn't bother leaving a note. No one ever noticed her missing anymore, anyway.

AUGUSTUS CLOSED THE OFFICE DOOR BEHIND Evangeline.

"Hey, I know we spent a lot of months alone, but people work here, now."

Evangeline slammed a piece of paper on his desk with one hand. "Explain this. Now."

"Move your hand, and I'll try," he said.

She pulled her arm back and crossed it over her chest with the other one. "I didn't ask you to do this."

"Give me a moment to figure out what we're talking about." He smoothed out the letter.

"MIT!" she yelled. "You sent in an application for me, don't deny it."

Augustus breathed out. He leaned back in his chair. "I won't deny it."

"I don't need your charity! Your... your persuasion! You don't think I could have been accepted on my own?"

"I know you could have, Evangeline." In that moment, she didn't only remind him of Madeline, with all her passions and heart, she *was* Madeline.

"So you did it anyway? So now I have to wonder whether they see me as an equal or a charity case?"

"I *didn't*," he said. "I didn't have to."

"Didn't have to what?"

"You might be surprised to learn they already knew who you were," Augustus said. "They're told about the best students in the nation, and you were on a list. The dean knew who you were immediately when I called."

"You did call, then."

"I did," he conceded. "But I didn't need to do anything. You had a place waiting for you long before I asked about it."

Evangeline flopped down in the seat on the other side of the desk. "Why?"

"Why did I call?"

Evangeline bit her lip. Her fist clenched and relaxed, over and over, in her lap. He didn't know what was going on in her mind. When she nodded, her wild hair bounced around her face.

Augustus searched for the answer closest to her surface. He couldn't go any deeper, not safely. "I see your potential, and I know... I know why you've stayed. But it's time for you to think of yourself, Evie. You're so smart. You have such a bright future ahead. It's time to look forward."

"Like you did?"

He wouldn't apologize for leaving the family home. Not even to his sister, who might be the only one who still needed him. "We all have to find our way to move on. You knew before I even asked you what you wanted. I didn't hand it to you, Evangeline. I nudged you forward on the path you were always supposed to be on."

Evangeline's head dropped, and when he saw her hair shake, he realized she was crying.

"Hey, it's okay," he said.

"It's not the letter."

He hardly heard her through the veil of hair.

"Evangeline?"

Her eyes were bright red when she looked up. "You have no idea what I've been through."

Augustus' stomach clenched. "I miss her, too."

"No, that's just the beginning for me. You don't know what's happened since."

Augustus inhaled. He'd known something was wrong with her. First, when she started hanging out with those kids on Dauphine, and later, when she stopped. He'd never asked her why. He'd been so busy with his own problems, so deep in his own head. "You can tell me," he offered.

"You think you mean well, and I know you do, Aggie. I know you. I know the only reason Madeline wasn't lost to us sooner was because you loved her the way you did. You were the only one who ever tried to understand her, and you paid the biggest price," Evangeline said. The words came out like mud over gravel, heavy and thick. "I came here to help you, and I guess I didn't realize how much I needed help, too. And then I got mixed up in something, and I played out the odds and... and I made the wrong decision. I should have come to you, and... if not before, then after, but I've never been so afraid, or so alone, in my whole life."

Augustus leaned forward. His hands were trembling in his lap. He wouldn't lose another sister. "Come home with me. Magnolia Grace is huge. You'll have your own space, but you won't have to be alone."

Evangeline's head shook wildly. "I was raped by four men, Augustus. Four men, who raped me in anger, for something I didn't do, because they felt entitled to hurt me when I couldn't protect myself."

The stark, naked truth of her words sent a shock through him, piercing him to his seat. He opened his mouth to speak, but nothing came out except a desperate cry. His blood pressure dropped so fast spots speckled the room around him.

"I relive it every day of my life. I wake in the middle of the night and feel their weight on top of me. I can smell the whiskey and grass on their breath. I can hear the girl, that horrible girl, Serenity, cheering them on, laughing, encouraging them to be rougher. I can't escape it and going away to college won't change anything. I'll still be the girl who couldn't fight back."

All the warmth in his body escaped through his skin. He was cold, a thousand pounds of ice. Tethered to the terrible truth she'd laid at his feet.

"Them all," he said through a heavy, cracked voice. The words came out backward. "I'll kill them all."

Evangeline wiped her eyes. "Don't you understand? Charles doing that is why that happened to me."

Augustus' blood cooled further as the truth bloomed into a clearer picture. He'd gone to Colleen for help, and she'd delegated the task to Charles, knowing full well, *full well*, what he might do with the information.

"Come home with me," he pleaded again. He didn't know how to fix this one. He couldn't go back in time for her, any more than he'd been able to do so for Madeline, and this failure weighed even harder than the first. "Come home with me, Evangeline."

"There's no home for me in this world anymore, Aggie." She stood and regarded him with a hard look. "Not here. Not in Massachusetts. Not anywhere. Not anymore."

She raced out the door before he could stop her. He jumped up and leaped around the desk, across the fallen chair left in her wake. But she was gone.

Augustus pulled at his hair, at the roots. What had he told himself, after Maddy was gone, and the dust had settled? When he could think again?

You believed you were the only one who could help her, and that fallacy contributed to her downward spiral.

He reached across his desk and yanked on the phone. His fingers ripped at the dial on the rotary, and he tapped his foot as he waited for an answer.

Elizabeth answered on the fourth ring. "Deschanel residence, state your purpose."

"Lizzy, I need Colleen. Now."

"Augustus?"

"Now!"

"Well, she's not here." Her voice dropped. "Are you okay?"

"I'm fine. Where is she? I need to know now!"

"Class," Elizabeth said. "Are you sure you're fine?"

"I'll be fine when I talk to Colleen." He pressed the plastic receiver, slamming it repeatedly until a dial tone appeared again.

He called the operator and asked to be put through to Tulane. Minutes later, he was on with one of the office secretaries, who seemed completely baffled by his request.

"Do you know how big this campus is?"

"Then you better get started."

Augustus waited ten minutes, then fifteen. When finally a voice appeared again on the other end, it was a very confused Colleen.

"What is this about? Is it Mama? Ophelia?"

"Evangeline," he said, out of breath though he'd not moved from his chair. "I need you to put aside your differences, and I need you to do it *right now*. I don't care what she did, it's not worth losing her."

"Losing her?" Colleen repeated. Then, after a pause, "I'm listening."

"This isn't one more thing for you to offload to Charles."

Colleen's voice was stiffer when she replied, "Fine."

"I thought she needed me, but who she needs is her sister. You're her best friend, Colleen, and I'm way out of my league. Last time I was out of my league, we lost Madeline." With the words out, a sob choked him.

"Don't say that. Don't *ever* say that. That is not on you," Colleen said. "Where is she now?"

"I don't know for sure, but I think she went home, and I think if she's left alone we might regret that."

He quickly told her what Evangeline confessed to him, and once she promised she was on her way to Vacherie, he cradled the phone and closed his eyes. He needed to breathe, now that he was alone. To compose himself so he, too, could head home to Ophélie.

Augustus didn't know how long he sat like that, but he was jolted alert by a knock on his office door.

Carolina shyly stepped through. He hadn't seen her in several weeks, not since he'd left her in his bed.

"I don't suppose you wanna see me, but I've given you space and now I have some things to say to you, and I'm not going to leave until you've listened."

Augustus nodded. He didn't have the energy to turn her away.

"I'm not mad," she said. "I'm confused. I was there, too, and for several hours I feel like I saw the real you."

"This is the real me," he said. "Focused. Alone."

"It's who you want to be, because it's safer."

He bristled at the suggestion. "Not everyone loves talking about their feelings, Carolina."

"Did you listen to anything I said that night? You're the only one I've ever told about Daniel, and what that did to me. I know the appeal of safe."

Augustus threw out his hands. "Maybe this is a safer life for me. It doesn't change anything. It's my choice."

Carolina came around his desk. She knelt before him and took his hands in hers. She pressed them to her face, then kissed them. "You think so little of yourself, when I think the world of you."

"You don't even know me," Augustus said, but his heart ached at her touch, which brought him back to when he was most open. Most vulnerable.

"There's many ways to know someone," she said softly. "I know you in the best way."

Augustus stood, and her hands fell away. "It isn't you. I just don't have anything to offer anyone. You deserve so much more than someone like me can give you."

"You don't want to open yourself to someone."

"Can't, or won't, there's no difference, and this won't end with anything other than me breaking your heart, and I don't want to hurt you, Carolina."

"My heart is already broken," she said, standing. She wiped her hands on her skirt and straightened her spine. "It was broken when I met you. It will stay that way, like yours. I just thought we would put our broken hearts together and make something a little less broken."

"I'm no good for you."

"As long as you believe that, you won't be good for yourself, either." She stretched on her toes and kissed him. "But I said what I came to say, Augustus. I hope you find your peace."

CHAPTER 17

You Can Close Your Eyes

Maureen lost her focus every other sentence. She didn't see the point in reading books. They were just words, lots of words, they weren't real and people who said books were an escape were the worst kind of fools. All books ended. You couldn't hide from reality forever.

Elizabeth attacked the assignment with fervor. She was almost finished, and they weren't even supposed to be halfway through. Complaining to her mother did nothing but make matters worse.

If you were on the same level as the state curriculum I'm supposed to be teaching you, you'd be reading different books.

Maureen could always count on her mother to remind her of her failings.

Great Expectations, the book was called, but she failed to see how the poor boy and his spoiled rich girlfriend made for great literature.

"Why, Maureen?" Peter asked as she groaned and threw the book across the room for the tenth time.

"It's no Shakespeare," she agreed. Madeline and August looked at the discarded book with pathetic expressions. Useless, both of them.

All of them.

A baby—her baby, another baby, it no longer mattered—cried in the distance in enthusiastic agreement.

You still have all that money from Virgins Only Club. It's more than you'll ever have until you get your trust. You could...

Nothing. She could do nothing. This world was not designed for young women on their own.

There was one character from the book she was not nearly so annoyed with, and as the story went on, her focus improved whenever Miss Havisham was on the page. Old, bitter Miss Havisham, roaming about her decrepit mansion in her rotting wedding gown, pining after her Compeyson. Now *that* was an image that made sense to Maureen. Was she not on that path? Doomed to be an old maid, her wealth irrelevant where it mattered most.

"Ah, yes, this drivel," Jean declared, turning his nose at the book splayed across the floor. "We tried to keep this from reaching our shores, but the Yankees and their ideas ruin everything."

"Pip," said Fitz. "Pip!"

"Hush, you fool."

Jean's snide comment, as with all his words, was unwelcome, but it did blossom into an idea... a wonderfully delicious idea, perhaps the best Maureen had experienced since moving to this old tomb.

The attic. She'd never been up there, because if anything in the world was haunted, it would be that dark, musty room forgotten by time.

Like Miss Havisham.

Maureen leaped off her bed with an energy she'd forgotten was possible.

"What are you up to?" Madeline asked, suspicious.

Maureen didn't answer her.

She went off in search of an old wedding dress.

Colleen, never the breaker of rules, broke every law, both the ones she knew and didn't know about, to get home.

New Orleans to Vacherie was an hour without traffic, and her cautious driving often added even more time. She did it in forty-five minutes.

Her car came to an abrupt stop several feet short of the front porch. She was jerked forward. As she came back, she nearly fell from the car after releasing her seat belt. She ran to the house, realizing she'd left her car door open, but she left it flapping and heaved open the door to Ophélie.

Irish Colleen appeared in the foyer. Her hands were covered in flour. "I wasn't expecting you home so early."

"My afternoon classes were cancelled," Colleen lied, breaking yet another rule. She brushed the stray hair off her face, praying her mother didn't see through to the truth.

"Shepherd's pie for dinner," her mother replied and returned to the kitchen.

Colleen raced up the stairs, tripping halfway up. She lost a shoe and kept moving, hobbling in her new, uneven gait.

Evangeline's door was unlocked. Colleen darted around the empty room, searching under the bed and in the closet. Her heart sank into her feet. She imagined finding her in her bed, reading, yelling at her to get out of her room already.

Colleen stopped outside the bathroom door. Steam traveled up and under the door. Her shoe-less foot squished in the damp carpet. With a jagged intake of breath, she went to turn the handle and wasn't surprised to find it locked.

She strained on her tiptoes, feeling up around the top of the doorframe. Her mother had hid the key there for years, making the idea of any real privacy an illusion, like so many other things.

Colleen closed her eyes and slipped the key in.

What she saw next turned her into someone else altogether. She compressed her horror at the scene, stuffing it deep into the compartments of her brain where such things went.

But she opened another that she'd closed not so long ago.

Colleen kicked through the flooded bathroom and dropped to her knees at the side of the tub. Evangeline's arm dangled, streams of red upon soft flesh, dripping into the current created by Colleen's intrusion.

"Evie, I'm here. I'm here. I'm here."

Colleen didn't look at Evangeline's face. She couldn't. To do so would send open all the compartments keeping her sane, and she had to be strong for her sister. Failing her was no longer an option, and really, it never had been.

She hadn't done this in so long, but it was like riding a bike. You never forgot the rush of power flowing through your palms and into the one in need. The sensation was almost erotic in its unbridled intimacy, and there was nothing Colleen could compare it to, nothing that came close to capturing the connection forged when she healed.

Colleen trembled as she held tight to her sister. Evangeline was alive, but her pulse had slowed to blips of intermittent energy, and the transfer of blood to and from her heart was inconsistent. Soon, if she didn't focus, it would stop altogether, and there'd be nothing she could do.

"You won't die, Evie. I won't allow it," Colleen whispered. The force of her energy sent her reeling backward and she settled on her heels. Tears threatened to break through the corners of her eyes, but she willed them away. They had no place here, where there was only her greatest regret transferred into something bigger: a promise.

"I promise you, you'll survive this," Colleen said, louder now, the words more real as she found her voice. "I've got you, Evangeline, and I'm never leaving again."

Evangeline moaned in her fitful streaming in and out of consciousness. Beneath Colleen's hands, her sister's flesh grew so warm she almost let go. But she doubled down on the force of her grip and grimaced as she pushed as hard as she'd ever done, healing through the combined force of her gift and her love.

When it was over, she pulled Evangeline's limp, wearied body from the bathtub and cradled her in her arms. Evangeline's soft sounds eventually turned to words when her eyes fluttered open.

"Leena..."

"You don't have to say anything. I know what happened, and I'm here now, and I'm never, ever going again," Colleen vowed. Now that her sister was safe, now that she was certain of this, the tears flowed. Several more compartments long closed re-opened. "I was stubborn and awful, and I'll never be sorry enough for it."

"It hurts so much." Evangeline's voice was a whisper, hoarse from the trauma. "I don't know what to do with the hurt when it becomes too much. I'm too logical for this. I only know of one way to dull what hurts too much to process."

Colleen crushed her sister to her chest. She rocked them in the water. "I can't heal that, Evie, but I can give you a place for the pain."

Evangeline sobbed in her arms, rolling herself inward.

"Evie, I mean it. I promise you, here and now, that no matter what passes between us in the future, I'll never turn my back on you. There's nothing you could do that's bigger than the loss of my life without you."

"I'm sorry about Rory," Evangeline mumbled. "I'm a freak. I don't know how to talk about things, and then bad things happen."

"You're my favorite freak," Colleen soothed. "The best person I know. We'll put our heads together and figure this out. We'll figure it out, Evie. I promise you."

"I didn't do this so you'd come," Evangeline said. She wrapped her arms around herself and nestled closer to Colleen.

"I know." Colleen kissed her hair. "But I did come, and now things will be different."

Two hours later, with Evangeline sound asleep in her bed, Colleen went to her sister's desk and wrote five names on a sheet of paper. She almost left off the name of the young woman, but her gender did not exempt her from the horror of her crime.

Charles waited in the hall. He wore the stoic, shell-shocked look of a man who had seen war and was ready for whatever else lay ahead.

Colleen walked by him with her hand outstretched.

Charles pressed his palm to hers, transferring the responsibility. He didn't look at the names before tucking the paper into his pocket and didn't ask her any questions.

Colleen felt no remorse in the act. She didn't tell herself he might just try a softer approach, to help herself sleep at night. She knew what would happen, and she saw no use in pretending her intentions, and the outcome, were anything but what they were.

They each had their roles to play in this family.

CHAPTER 18

Two Sides of the Coin

Charles finished off the last of his Dixie beer. He shook it, upside down, over his mouth, and then tossed the empty can into the backseat. The paper bag on his passenger seat was empty, save for the discarded ring that held the six-pack together when he'd brought it earlier. He should have bought two. He'd remember that for next time. Each time brought new lessons.

He *was* getting better at this. His first was a haphazard, sloppy mess born of his rage. Completely justifiable rage, he told himself at the time, and even now, but rage didn't keep men out of prison, and one day Augustus would meet a judge he couldn't manipulate.

The second, that good-for-nothing Ethan Summerland, wasn't easier, but it was simpler. He knew when he left the house what he'd come to do, whereas with that shitbag Evers he'd convinced himself, right up until the moment of truth, that he was there just to talk.

He hadn't said anything at all to Evers; to Ethan, only this: My sisters are off-limits.

Ethan, sitting on his couch in his boxers, measuring his grass on that ridiculous ivory scale he was so proud of, died wearing the same dumb look he'd perfected in life.

Charles had gotten one thing right about his first act as protector. The Maurepas swamp was easy to get in and out of, but the only visitors were locals, for there were better spots for the hard-core sportsmen, and more accessible places for the tourism industry. The old Cajuns parked their trucks along the road to drop their lines and nets out there, but the bayou was unrelenting to anything foreign. They'd only ever find catfish and sac-a-lait. Evers *had* been found, but the swamp had eaten away any shred of evidence. He dropped Summerland even farther into the swamp, and guessed he was lost to the ecosystem.

The police had never connected the dots on Evers or Summerland. Just as they would not connect them with what he was fixing to do tonight.

His other learning was patience.

Two weeks had passed since Colleen slipped him the names, two ships passing in the night. In those two weeks, he'd used his time to follow the five individuals who had wronged Evangeline, to learn their schedules. Relying on that fool Jared for help had been a grave miscalculation during the whole Evers debacle. Had he known how it would end, he would've never involved someone else. It was sloppy, and he'd since learned that it set off a chain of events leading him to where he now sat, in the car, across the street from the abandoned house. Jared had told others how he'd investigated Evers for Charles, and some of those others connected the pattern when Summerland went missing. That pattern led to the assault on Evangeline.

He couldn't forgive himself, but he could fix this.

Charles could pick them off, one by one, but their string of disappearances would raise far more eyebrows than what he had planned.

Charles needed all five of them together, but he couldn't risk others being present as well. Vengeance was one thing. Any collateral damage would make this murder, plain and simple.

The girl, Serenity, whose name was about to become highly ironic, was apparently more than just a casual enthusiast of gang rape. She was also aces at stealing food, and tonight, she'd invited her four conspirators to a feast. Charles had watched in strange fascination as she slipped in and out of the various restaurants along Bourbon and Royal, camouflaged in her white cook's outfit, stealing a plate here and a plate there until her cart was full. She pulled it along, down to the river, along the levee toward the Bywater.

Serenity pulled the cart up from the sidewalk and into an overgrown yard. She tugged it, walking backward as she yanked it over the debris littering the ground. One by one, she moved the plates from the cart to the porch, and when she was done, she was off again, possibly to retrieve more contraband for her dinner party for five.

Charles would never know. He had no plans to follow her, this time. He had to work fast, because he didn't know how long she'd be gone.

He swung open the door to his Trans Am and looked around, cigarette dangling. He took one last long hit of smoke and then flicked it away, into the night. The whole neighborhood was a remnant of something that once was, but no longer. Boarded windows and weeds had claimed the homes and, aside from the graffiti decorating the boards and peeling paint, there were no signs of life. The abandoned old grade school at the end of the block stood sentry over the whole sad mess.

Charles slinked through the street, reminding himself to stay always aware. No one of importance lived in these homes, but the homeless, like Serenity and her band of thugs, might be camping out. They probably wouldn't snitch to the police—if he'd learned one valuable thing from that wretch Summerland, it was that the homeless trusted the police less than they trusted their enemies—but Augustus would murder *him* if he had to solicit his help with this one.

The cans of gasoline bounced off his legs as he ran. Gas sloshed out the top, dripping out onto the street. When he stumbled into the yard, he made for the back.

He wished he'd paid more attention in chemistry, or he

would've been able to come up with something more creative than gasoline. For the briefest moment of panic, he wondered if the police would see this for the obvious arson job it was, but he calmed, realizing the police didn't care about these neighborhoods. They were forgotten to time, and the homeless, just one more, or less, problem.

Charles hunched down as he sprinkled the flammable liquid around the base of the house, splashing it up against the wood siding as he worked his way around the foundation. When the first can was empty, he chucked it over the broken-down fence of the neighboring property. He took the second can and slipped through the back of the house, which was not only unlocked but lacked a door entirely.

He was more careful here. He didn't want them to smell the gas right away and leave. Charles dug around in his pockets for the patchouli incense he'd bought earlier in the day. His following of the gang revealed their love of the disgusting scent, and he burned it now as he spread the rest of the gasoline around the backs of discarded furniture, and along baseboards.

From his back pocket, he pulled out the hammer and box of nails. He went around to each window and shored up their boards, making them all but impossible to pull off in a hurry.

After, Charles returned to the kitchen. The missing door could be a problem, but he saw the solution immediately. He pulled the stove off the floor where it had fallen to its side, righting it, and slid it over to the door, blocking the escape. If he could do this, they could as well, so he went to search for other appliances to stack on top and around it. Ten minutes later, the escape was blocked by a washer and dryer, and an armoire. He hoped it was enough.

No, he couldn't leave it like that. He ran out the front and returned to the backyard, searching for more boards, anything he could use to tack up the back door in case they managed to remove his block. He stacked old wood in his arms until he couldn't see a thing and went to work nailing them across the open back door until he was satisfied the work would hold.

When he was done, he ran back to his car. Still no sign of them, but his heart raced now, at the thrill... at the terror.

One by one, he removed the cement blocks and carried them to the house. He piled them off to the side, where they wouldn't be seen, or stand out. The back end of his car sighed in relief. The ride home would be so much lighter.

Charles returned to the car and drove it around the block. He jogged back to the street, with a bottle and a rag in hand, and hid behind a bush on the other side of the road, waiting.

Laughter in the distance caught his attention. He peered around the jagged mess of thorns to see Serenity and her four men in tow, each carrying their share of bags and plates. Serenity's cart was there, too, but one of the others pulled it along now. Lackeys in life, and soon, in death.

Charles waited until they were inside, and then he darted back across the street.

Through a gap in the boards of a window, he watched and waited for them to settle in and get comfortable. When he was certain, he began moving the cement blocks in front of the front door, quietly, one by one.

He lit the gasoline-soaked rag sticking out of the bottle and said a quick prayer before launching it through another gap in the boards at the back of the house.

"For Evangeline," he said and waited.

If things went to plan, he could make it home in time to join his own family for Thanksgiving dinner.

Augustus heaved a heavy sigh as he stepped through the front door of Magnolia Grace. He hung his sport coat on the oak rack by the door and sighed again.

He had every reason tonight to be happy. To be celebrating. Deschanel Magazine's first volume was done and wrapped, and would hit newsstands on December 23. The whole town was talking about a magazine for New Orleans society, published by one of their own. Their box was overflowing with submissions for future editions. There was even talk of Augustus being the next King of Rex this coming Mardi Gras season, which was an honor so great he couldn't wrap his mind around it. Only the best men and women of New Orleans—and the richest—were named to the court of Rex. Some people went their whole lives vying for the roles.

It was also an honor he didn't want.

Augustus looked in the direction of the kitchen. He hadn't eaten a thing all day, and he knew he should be hungry… knew he should eat. If he was a good son, he'd be at Ophélie tonight, celebrating Thanksgiving. His absence would be noted. Irish Colleen would never bring it up, but he'd see it in her eyes, where she wore her truths most clearly. She'd never chide him with words. He was the good son. *You should have been heir.* But oh, how grateful he was that he'd been born second and not been forced into such a role. He was the compliant one; the one who would do anything for his family if asked. But he no more had what it took to lead this family than Charles did.

His footsteps boomed over the old cypress flooring. A reminder it was only him in this massive estate, which had been built for the warmth of a large family. Augustus struggled to imagine a future where he entered through this door to be greeted by a kiss from his wife. Where kids squealed and ran to wrap their arms around his legs.

Augustus dropped his briefcase in the center of the floor. He found he didn't have the energy to take it to his office, where it belonged. It was as out of place as he was at Magnolia Grace.

He shuffled across the floor, hardly able to hold his own weight. With one hand, he gripped the bannister, but as his feet started to ascend the steps, he realized with alarm he'd forgotten something important. The most important.

Augustus went to the dresser by the door. The graveyard of candles burned down to their base had grown over time. They dotted the landscape around the silver-framed picture of Madeline. He liked this one, because she wasn't looking at the camera. She hadn't even known the picture was being taken, so the photographer—Elizabeth, he thought, but couldn't be certain—had captured her in a moment between the anguish. Where she'd been just Maddy, not the woman determined to take on the whole world's pain.

Augustus struck a match against the side of the box and lit a fresh candle. He blew on the match and tossed it in the small bowl on the right of the table, where all the discarded matches went to rest.

"Happy Thanksgiving, Maddy," he said and returned to the stairs, to the long ascension, to where his bed, and nothing else, no one else, greeted him.

CHAPTER 19

Never That Simple

Evangeline read about the accident in the Times Picayune. There was nothing remarkable about a house fire in the Bywater, but five young people, ages sixteen to twenty-seven, perished inside. Three had been registered as runaways for more than a year. Two were from good families.

She didn't let herself feel the joy creeping up from within her. This was only confirmation that Craig and the others had been right about her brother Charles all along. The paper mentioned the suspicion of arson, but they had no suspects, and they never would. If they even came close, Augustus would handle the authorities, as he so obviously had before.

So many things made sense now, and yet didn't at all.

That either Colleen or Augustus, the absolute last of her siblings she'd expect to condone or encourage violence and lawlessness, was responsible for activating Charles, left Evangeline hollow and uncertain.

If this didn't sum up her family, nothing did. Most of them were hardly close, but when one of their own was threatened, they transformed into a well-oiled machine of protection and retribution.

And where did that leave her? This revelation left her family divided into two groups in her mind: her older siblings on one side, her younger on the other. She fell more comfortably into the first group, but knowing what she knew now, she couldn't be one of them if she didn't find her role. And to find her role, she must first accept what had been done to protect her... to protect Maureen... to protect them all.

If she left in the spring, like Augustus wanted, she'd flounder on her own, searching for an individual meaning when to be a Deschanel was to be part of something bigger. Here it was again, that pesky Gestalt, reminding her that the sum of their parts was so much greater than their value as individuals.

Evangeline was torn between the precipice of these two worlds. Through one doorway lay the opportunity to reach her potential as Evangeline; through the other, her potential as a Deschanel.

Her coiled hair taunted her in the mirror. She could tie it back, or she could let it run free. The choice was so much more than it seemed. What had this moment been like for Colleen, when she decided to suppress her individual morals in favor of their collective conscience?

Everything in her life was a symbol now. Her inner scientist screamed. She craved clarity and absolutes. She could have them, and only fifteen hundred miles separated her from a life where nothing was without explanation.

Colleen appeared behind her in the mirror. She rested her face on Evangeline's shoulder, nesting in a tuft of her hair. Her arms wrapped around Evangeline's waist, drawing their hands together.

"We don't ever have to speak of it," Colleen said. "Unless you want to. But if you do, it's just the two of us. Just us girls. Charles and Augustus will never speak a word. That's how this works."

"Jerks. I have questions. This isn't some small thing, and now we just go about our lives as if..."

"You know them. Augustus will pretend nothing ever happened, and Charles will fly off the handle at even the subtlest implication against his character."

"How did you know?"

"What you were thinking?"

"Yes."

"Sister's intuition," Colleen said. She winked at their reflections. "We know who we are, Evangeline. That's more than most get in life."

"Monsters?"

"Is that what you think?" Colleen asked. "Truly?"

"No," Evangeline admitted. "I have so many questions."

"I have no satisfying answers."

"It won't end there, will it?" Evangeline asked. She squeezed her sister tighter, stretching her arms around them both.

"Probably not."

"How do you..."

"Sleep at night?" Colleen finished. She kissed her cheek, raised her head, and kissed the other. "Same way anyone does, when their family is safe."

Evangeline watched her carefully in the mirror. "It's not that simple, Leena."

"No," Colleen agreed. She nestled her face into her sister's hair and laid her head to the side. "It never is."

EVANGELINE WALKED THROUGH THE OFFICE OF Deschanel Media Group. Over thirty people worked there now, and they buzzed back and forth in a frenzy as the office approached the release of their first ever edition of Deschanel Magazine.

With a surprising shock of sentiment, Evangeline almost missed the days where the ceilings were exposed. Where Augustus cursed over that damned stack of insulation half-blocking the halls. Back then, it was theirs. Now, it was so much more.

She found him in his office. He had his reading glasses on and a red pen in his hand, as he read through something that had him in rapt attention. He didn't need the glasses, and she had always been so amused by whatever propelled him to wear them. It was as if somewhere inside him, he believed he must be older, more worn, more damaged to be considered successful.

"Aggie!" she barked when he didn't immediately notice her.

"Hi, hi," he said quickly. "Things are a zoo around here. Can I get you something?"

"If I need something, I can get it myself," she said, a touch sore at how easily the place had moved on without her. She was a part of the DNA, and she wanted to run out into the open office and scream, *Do you know who I am?*

He smiled. "Right. Of course. What's going on?"

"I just wanted to see you, that's all."

He nodded, with a growing look of suspicion. "I see. Irish Colleen didn't wrangle you into Christmas baking?"

"I'd as soon drown myself in the river," she quipped, but neither laughed, because that joke ceased to be funny when you'd tried to kill yourself for real.

It was then that Evangeline realized why Augustus had chosen December 23 to launch his magazine into the world. She was certain he would've launched it on Christmas Day, if he'd been able to convince the rest of the office to go along with working the holiday.

The preparation had him working around the clock. Kept him so busy he had no time to think, no time to remember the anniversary upon them.

"I don't have a lot of free time right now," he said and looked guilty. She wanted to reach forward and comfort him, reassure him that she wasn't in danger anymore, thanks to him. That he had saved her life, and she'd never take it for granted again.

Instead, she tried something else. "Aggie, Colleen said you'd never talk about any of it." His panicked eyes confirmed she didn't need to clarify "it." "And I'm not going to ask you to. I just wanted you to know that I know, and that I'm all in."

Augustus watched her with a curious expression. He sucked in his bottom lip and released it with a long exhale. "You're not going to MIT, are you?"

Evangeline shook her head. "Not right now. I stopped in at

Tulane admissions on the way here, and I'm starting there in the spring. I'll see how that goes."

He brightened. "So you are going back to school. That's great news."

"And I'd like to take you up on your offer."

"Which was?"

"To come live with you at Magnolia Grace," she said. "I'll pay rent. I'm not a freeloader."

Augustus snickered. "Don't be ridiculous. I didn't pay for that house, either."

"So you still want me, then?"

He looked away, to the side. Thinking. He returned his eyes to her and smiled. "Yeah, I still want you. Does Mama know?"

"Hell no!" Evangeline declared. "But she's been talking about moving out of Ophélie, too."

"What? Why?"

"She said Charles would need it soon," Evangeline replied. "Whatever that means."

Augustus leaned back in his chair, deep in thought. "I see."

"She has the Sullivans looking into townhomes back in New Orleans."

"Curious," Augustus said. "All right, then. I'll have a key made for you, and I'll bring it by Christmas Eve."

"Make it the twenty-third. You *are* coming to your party, right?"

Augustus pressed his lips tight. Everyone, even Irish Colleen knew, how little he actually wanted a party, let alone one focused on him. But she insisted on celebrating the milestone of the inaugural edition of Deschanel Magazine, and there were some battles you couldn't win with the woman.

"Please don't let the guest list get out of control."

"That's like you asking me to dam up the Mississippi with my bare hands."

He groaned. "One night," he muttered. "I suppose we can survive one night."

Evangeline nodded. She looked around the Spartan room. No

signs of life, of personality. No pictures, no keepsakes. At some point, he'd either discarded or moved the misguided sign from Carolina.

I miss Maddy, too, Aggie. Every day. Every single damn day.

"I'll see you soon," Evangeline said as she pulled herself out of the chair.

AUGUSTUS PEEKED HIS HEAD OUT OF THE OFFICE LATER that night. There was only one other employee still hanging around at this late hour, and she was new.

Two weeks prior, Colin's father, also named Colin, had called from Sullivan & Associates. One of their associate attorneys, Joseph Connelly—Cat's uncle—had asked Colin for help in placing the girl, a Soviet immigrant they'd hired for something else, and learned she lacked any of the skills required. But, apparently, she had other, more valuable skills.

Augustus had met with Joseph for coffee.

"She came to us as an au pair, but she's *awful* with children," Joseph had said, shaking his head with a grin. "With people in general, actually. I think she signed up for this because it's what all her friends were doing to get to the United States. But it's really not her thing."

"Why should I take her?" Augustus had laughed. How did he get chosen to relieve another man's burden?

"Because she *is* good at something. Really good. Accounting." Joseph took a swallow of his water with a guilty look and added, lowering his voice, "I put her through business school."

Augustus was incredulous. "You paid for this Soviet immigrant to go to business school?"

"Well, yes, I did," Joseph had replied, nonplussed. "It seemed like the right thing to do for a girl with such talent, and who'd gone to such obvious trouble to come here. Anyway, Colin says you're hiring for a junior accountant. I realize you have your reservations, and I might too in your position, but I can't recommend her enough, Augustus. I'm putting my name out here for this girl. I don't think you'll be disappointed."

Augustus didn't agree immediately, and also didn't take Joseph's word for it. He called the business school and asked for Ekatherina Vasilyeva's records. They gave him no hassle and were eager to tell him that she was their very best student. *Quiet girl. Never any trouble. We hope she can find a company to sponsor her. Would be such a shame if she was sent back to the USSR.*

This appealed to Augustus in a way even Joseph's endorsement hadn't. If anyone understood laboring quietly to build a new life, it was him.

He surprised even himself when he hired her without an interview, and when she showed up for her first day, he mistook her for a lost child. Ekatherina was a tiny thing, with pale blond hair and big blue eyes. Nearing her twenty-second birthday, according to the paperwork he held in his hands, but she didn't look a day over fifteen.

"Pleased to meet you, Ekatherina," he had said, taking her small hand in his. For such a delicate girl, her handshake was firm and took him by surprise.

"Please, call me Catherine," came the soft, mousy reply. Her accent was strong, but her English was crisp. *She's been preparing for this for years,* Joseph had said.

Catherine didn't seem right, either. She'd chosen this name as an escape from who she was born, just as Augustus had always shrugged off prestige of his own family name. Neither wanted to be who they were and had very clear visions of who they wanted to be. She was an enigma, but he understood this very fundamental thing about her and liked her immediately.

He'd sent her off to work in the three-man accounting department. The only woman, and the only immigrant. That she was Russian, a name that sent simultaneous anger and chills through many in the country, seemed to hold double the indictment.

But each day, when the chorus of metal clasps closing on briefcases sounded through the office at just past six, Ekatherina—

Catherine, though he couldn't bring himself to call her this, just as he'd never completely thrown aside his own name—showed no signs of stopping. Long after half the lights had been turned down, and the din of a bustling office died to a quieter lull of evening, she was there, head down, with her adding machine and pencil.

Augustus glanced back at the clock. It was nearing eleven. He shouldn't keep burning the midnight oil like this; he knew it, and yet he felt more at home here than home itself. It was safe. It was his.

Did Ekatherina feel the same way? Was this where she was safe to be herself?

He slipped his arms into his tweed jacket and tugged on the leather of his suitcase. He locked the door to his office and meandered through the growing villages of cubicles that had popped up to support his business.

Augustus stopped at her desk. When she didn't immediately look up, he cleared his throat and shifted his briefcase from one hand to another.

"Going home?" she asked, one finger still poised over the nine on her adding machine. He nearly smiled. Her words were perfunctory. Her mind was elsewhere.

"I'll be locking up the office on the way out."

"Oh. I see." Her face fell, and her hand with it. She made a notation in her notebook, and then closed it.

"Can I walk you out?"

She appeared to think about it for a moment. Then she slipped her purse over her shoulder and stood. "Yes, thank you, Mr. Deschanel." She had no jacket, and he nearly offered his, when he remembered that what was cold for someone from New Orleans was likely balmy for a Russian.

"Augustus," he corrected.

Ekatherina gave him the same look he had probably given when she told him to call her Catherine. *I'm not calling you Augustus any more than you'll call me Catherine.*

She followed him out and waited patiently as he locked up the office doors. They descended the stairs in silence, and when they stepped into the quiet night of the Central Business District, it occurred to him that this was the last time they would see one another until the New Year. Deschanel Media Group was closed until the New Year, to allow for family time. It hadn't been his idea—Evangeline was often the heart behind the operation, reminding him of the things he should know but didn't.

"Can I drop you off somewhere?"

"I have a car, Mr. Deschanel."

"Yes. Of course." Augustus again shifted his briefcase. He should say something else. And then he remembered. "Merry Christmas, Ekatherina. Do you have family here?"

"Merry Christmas, Mr. Deschanel," she answered, flashing a polite but distant smile. "And I will be just fine. Thank you for asking."

Ekatherina nodded and disappeared into the night.

CHAPTER 20

Stairway to Heaven

Maureen finished the book. She set it aside, but the effects lingered, coursing through her. She *was* Miss Havisham; younger, yes, but the cruelty of life did not discriminate by age.

Maureen wanted to run through the house and stop all the clocks, as Miss Havisham had done in Satis House. She envisioned serving herself as the final course of Christmas dinner so that they may all feed upon her physically as they had done metaphorically.

Oh, if only she'd known reading could be like this!

But it was no escape. No, not that. No, this book, *Great Expectations*, had instead shown her the way to interpret all the darkness festering upon her soul like so many rabid mice. Like Miss Havisham, many had pretended to love her, from duty, like her family, or from desire, as the degenerate Mr. Evers had... as the boys had. Her invitation or acquiescence did not lessen the crimes against her.

Her voyage into the attic had not been a disappointment. Her ghosts had even left her alone when she ascended the old stairs in the dark corner of the hall. Maybe it was too haunted even for them.

Maureen found trunks and trunks of old clothing, deliciously romantic pieces with high collars and frills for days. She wanted to drag them all down and play dress-up, for there was no crime against pretending to be someone else... a kidnapped heiress trapped in a tower awaiting rescue... an escaped debutante who joined the carnival, only to find love with the lion tamer. She could still be Miss Havisham, and still be these other things, because if her ghosts had taught her anything, it was that the only escape to be found was within your own imagination.

She found what she'd been in search of in the trunk with the gold label, the words *Amelia Cutright Bridal Trunk.* This was her grandmother's, and though she had never met her, Maureen felt a magnetic pull to the contents inside, as if they were linked through the generations. As if Amelia whispered across space and time, *These are yours now, child.*

Maureen had never cared so much about her family's past as when she held it in her hands. Oh, to see the pictures! Had they wed here at Ophélie, under the ancient oaks? That seemed right. Felt right.

As luck—no fate, she didn't believe in luck—would have it, the dress fit her as well as if she'd had it tailored for her. She squeezed it around her tiny curves, slipping her arms into the satin sleeves.

And then she hung it at the back of her closet, awaiting the perfect time.

She finished the book on December 23. In a couple hours, the guests would begin arriving for Augustus' celebration party. The whole thing was ridiculous. Augustus was the last person on earth who would ever want such a thing, but no one in this family cared what others thought when they made decisions. Irish Colleen went about planning the whole soiree as if it were only her feelings that mattered.

Maureen imagined herself descending the staircase in her grandmother's wedding gown, all eyes drawn to the spectacle of the Deschanel debutante swimming in ruffles and rotting hand-spun lacework.

It was a horrid idea, and it was a perfect idea. She smiled to herself, but the smile dropped from her face at the terrible realization that her only joys in life were found in hurting others.

No, she would have to miss out on the delicious shock on the guests' faces. Her mother would corner her then and there, and the rest of her plan would be forfeit. She couldn't risk it, not when she'd been planning it for months, and every day that passed, with the dead whispering in one ear and screaming in the other, brought her further confidence that this was the only way.

Maureen laid the old gown, which was no longer truly white after years of withering away in the attic, across her bed.

Tonight, she would wear the dress in earnest and float across Satis House, in search of the truth.

She would go where it led.

Charles leaned into the massive column on the front portico of Ophélie. He stubbed his cigarette on the heel of his shoe and turned against the old plaster, knowing he was needed inside.

He found he couldn't make himself budge. Everyone would be there tonight, thanks to his mother. She'd invited Colin, though he was the last person Charles wanted to see. No, he'd be *bringing* the last person he wanted to see. And he'd have to smile and pretend he was happy for them. He'd have to endure her showing her ring to all the women who couldn't help but be interested, whether they were actually interested or not. Men got a lot of shit for being cads, but women were the queens of deception.

Catherine Connelly would become Catherine Sullivan in 1973, and Charles couldn't help but feel it was a move born of revenge. *I don't love him like that,* she had assured him, whenever his own guilt moved to the forefront of the arrangement. *He's more like a brother. I would do anything for him, but he doesn't have my heart.*

Hindsight taunted him, reminding him he could have read her mind and discovered her deception long before he'd given his heart away. But he'd never been very good at it, and maybe that was because he understood, deep down, if someone wanted you to know what they thought of you, they'd tell you.

Colin still didn't know anything. He didn't have to, because Rory had only threatened to spill if Cat didn't cut off ties with Charles. For days, Charles agonized over the inevitable phone call or visit from Colin. He practiced what he would say, but everything came up so woefully short of anything even vaguely resembling justification.

Days passed, and then weeks, and he knew he'd never have to say anything at all.

And then Colin showed up at his doorstep, beaming a smile bigger than any Charles had ever seen him wear. He wanted to ask him in person to be his best man. He couldn't think of anyone else, not his brothers, anyone he wanted to stand by him more.

"I never thought she'd come back. I tried everything," Colin said, that day, a week past. "I thought for a while she'd met someone."

The devil living inside Charles, the one who had pushed him in a single direction for most of his life, wanted so badly to tell him. How he'd fucked her until she screamed. How she felt when she came beneath him.

"I'm happy for you, man." He'd taken this one as a quiet victory. Lying had never been his strength, but Colin bought it.

But then, why wouldn't he? Why would he ever suspect Charles, of all people, to have been the reason she stayed away?

The sun painted the river red and orange. In an hour, the house would be all laughter and bright lights, Irish Colleen playing the role of hostess better than she'd ever played the role of mother.

On second thought, Charles lit another cigarette. He slipped the bottle of cognac out of his inner jacket pocket and broke the seal.

MAUREEN, STILL IN HER OWN CLOTHES, MOVED QUIETLY through the house, slipping past relatives, servants, invisible, as always. One by one, she changed the clocks to five past ten, the moment at which she had given up her child and surrendered herself to the fate chosen for her. The living dead.

She should be out of the house before the first of the guests arrived. She had no patience for their inevitable questions, which she would not begin to answer for the rest of the world existed on one plane, and she another. They were not on her level.

Maureen slipped into the dress for the second time. She fastened all the tiny pearl buttons herself, careful not to tug at the fabric too hard. Many hung by fraying threads, and she hadn't mended any of them, as she should have.

She let her long, wavy hair hang free. The waves from her braids the night before had a hint of Hollywood glamour, and she admired herself a moment longer before she left her room. She was a vision, as Miss Havisham had surely been a vision when she'd first worn her own dress, only to be jilted.

Maureen took the servant's stairs, so she could disappear out the back. Several of the staff did double takes when she floated by, but only Layla stopped her.

"Miss Maureen, you shouldn't take that beautiful dress outside, not when it's been raining."

"Oh, it's been raining? Even better!" She ran off, cackling, leaving the poor housemaid with a list of questions.

Maureen lifted the dress to keep the hem from dragging through the mud, but on second thought, let it sweep across the grass and collect whatever it may, just as Miss Havisham had not stopped her own dress from decaying as she did.

She made it across the long lawn, all the way to the hedges that shielded Ophélie from the prying eyes of passing cars. She looked both ways, twice, before crossing River Road and ascending the grass-covered levee.

Maureen reached the top. From here, the Mississippi raged to her left. Ophélie, all her acreages, all her glory, spread out in all directions to the right.

She threw her arms out and her head back and spun in lazy

circles as the rain pummeled her face, her hands. It soaked her dress, and she laughed and laughed and laughed.

The storm pushed on harder, until she could pretend her tears were just raindrops, and that everything was just as it should be.

CHARLES WENT TO LIGHT UP ANOTHER SMOKE WHEN HE saw the figure in white darting across the lawn from the side of the house.

He must be hallucinating. There was no way a woman in a wedding dress was running across his property. But he'd had no hallucinogens today, and not nearly enough Hennessy for alcohol to be behind the strange vision.

Charles strained to make sense of what he was seeing. Then he knew.

He knew *who*.

But he couldn't fathom *why*.

He set the bottle on the steps and headed down the driveway.

MAUREEN COLLAPSED AT THE DOCK. NO SHIPS WOULD arrive here, not anymore. The river had been a different animal in the days the pier was built, at least that's what her father used to say, when he was a man of flesh and bone and not a specter haunting her days and nights.

She extended a hand down toward the water, but she was nowhere close to touching the surface. The level was high today, probably from the storms. The end of the sleeve formed a lacy V over the top of her dainty hand, and she thought, oh how lovely this is. How lovely I feel.

Maureen practiced falling forward and catching herself. She gasped in delight at how close she came to tumbling into the river, which was unusually still for this time of day. Normally the passage was filled with barges and tankers en route to... wherever they went.

She remembered a picture Mr. Evers had displayed on the

projector in his classroom. Most of the students passed notes during his Shakespeare lectures, and Maureen was no exception, but she shooed away the distractions when this image came up.

The greens on the banks, shrouding the lovely Ophelia, drowned of her own pain. Her dress was not so very different from the one Maureen wore now, though in her hands was wound the most vivid flora, reds and yellows and blues. Ophelia, hands turned up to receive her next life.

Maureen interpreted this to be a more symbolic death for the angelic Ophelia, who had seen too much in her life to be expected to continue as she had. Ophelia allowed the image of herself, the one seen and expected by others, to die while she, herself lived on.

It was a more hopeful ending than Miss Havisham's, but Maureen didn't have the heart to burn down the family mansion.

She didn't want to die, in any case. She'd seen the dead and knew there was no peace for them, either. But there had to be another way... any way... and as she gazed down at the mucky reeds poking up from the riverbank, she saw the way.

Maureen, blinded by her tears, closed her eyes and pitched forward.

Her breath caught as strong arms caught her around the waist. Her first thought was that her ghosts had grown beyond their limitations, but then she was stumbling back, the smell of some strong liquor swirling in the air between her and her savior.

"Maureen, what the *hell* are you doing?" Charles demanded. He released her, but his arms stayed extended, as if expecting her to leap into the river anyway if he gave her too much freedom.

Maureen sniffled and spun in her dress, but the energy and enigma of the idea had dissolved with the first touch of reality. Her arms fell to her sides. "This is my life now."

"What are you talking about?" He stepped as she stepped, moving with her. "Why are you out here, and *what the fuck are you wearing*?"

Maureen started to explain everything, but all her energy

drained into the ground beneath her and she collapsed into a heap of satin and taffeta.

Charles ran his hands over his wet hair. He looked around, shook his head, and then fell down on his heels. "Come on, let's get you back, okay?"

Maureen's head shook furiously. She refused to look at him. "I can't go back. I can't go back there, or anywhere."

"Don't be silly," he said. He tugged at her hand and she pulled it right back, dropping it in her lap. "Augustus' party is starting any minute now."

Maureen whipped her head up. "Do you think I care about that? About a party? About anything at all?"

"Shit, Maureen, do you think I do?"

The rain picked up, and with it, the wind. Charles pulled his jacket off and draped it over her head, a sad gesture. The thing was soaked. "You gonna tell me why you're out here, in... in *that*?"

"I don't have anyone for you to murder, so don't get your hopes up."

He smirked. He couldn't help it. "Pity."

"Not if you knew where the dead went."

"I've never cared about any of that. Heaven. Hell. Who cares? We have no choice, either way."

"It's not heaven or hell you have to worry about, you damn fool." She wiped her face with the taffeta.

"Look, we can have a philosophical discussion back at the house—"

"Stop talking to me like I'm a child! You don't know who I am, Charles! None of you do!"

This shut him up. He ran his hand over his chin. "So, tell me."

She glared through her tears. "Why should I?"

He lifted his shoulders. "Can you think of a good reason not to?"

"If only you knew..." She laughed, a cold, dark sound that echoed in the static air. "You'd know why I've never told anyone."

"Maureen, if there's anyone in this whole damn family who knows about secrets and bullshit, it's yours truly."

"This isn't drugs and whores, Huck."

"Hey, they're not all whores."

Maureen's mouth twitched. Of all her siblings, it should have been Charles who would understand her. She thought she could have even told him about the Virgins Only Club, and his most likely response would have been to give her pointers. He didn't stand on morals, or tradition. His honor was whatever he wanted it to be.

"You can tell me, which might feel good," Charles said. "Or, you can drown in that fucking awful dress and go wherever it is you think the dead go."

"Nowhere," she said, before she could stop herself. "They don't go anywhere."

"What makes you so sure? You seeing ghosts now? Did they tell you to wear that dress?"

Maureen smiled. There was no joy in the gesture, only a deep, sardonic disdain that might, just maybe, find relief in the unburdening.

She told him everything.

Charles didn't let Maureen go as they walked back to the house. His arm was slipped around her waist, under the jacket he'd draped over her shoulders.

What she'd told him blew his mind. It was fucking bananas. But Maureen didn't have the imagination for these kinds of lies. And whatever these ghosts had done to her over the years, she'd endured it alone.

He snuck her in the servant's door and escorted her up the back steps. When he was certain the upstairs hall was empty, he rushed her to her room, so she could change and wash away the craziness of the levee.

"Your secret is safe with me," he told her as she moved to close the door. "You don't have to do this alone anymore."

Maureen smiled, but her eyes were still dark. "We'll see, Huck."

"Mama, can we talk?"

"Now?" Irish Colleen had a dish in each hand and was heading into the formal dining room. "Everyone's seated at the table now. We're about to eat."

"It won't take long."

"All right," she said. She set the dishes aside, but left her hands in the mitts. "What is it, Charles?"

He didn't know how to find the words. Where to search for them. He'd never been much for anything serious and was convinced he'd said all the wrong things to Maureen, in a moment where he was certain the wrong words could be devastating.

But he would try. He couldn't lose another sister. Nor could he keep knocking off all the assholes who did them wrong.

"Well?" she asked, impatient. She looked behind her, toward the dining room.

"I want to redeem myself."

"You what?"

"To redeem myself," he said, louder this time. "I know I've failed the family. I know you think… that I'm a disgrace."

"Now, dear… that's not entirely true."

"It's true enough. I've failed at a lot of things, but there's one thing I can't fail at, because I don't have any choice. I'm the heir, and I need to do better."

Irish Colleen relaxed a bit. She nodded. "I wasn't expecting this, I have to say."

"I know," Charles said. "But I'm ready to settle down and lead this family, Mama. Tell me what I need to do. Whatever you say, I'll do it."

She exhaled and crossed her arms. "I've told you before, it's time for you to be married."

Charles' stomach turned. He felt Cat's soft, warm flesh again, pressed into his as she slept. He saw her eyes flash with pure, unbridled desire as he drove within her. "If that's what you think is best."

"I think it's best. For you too, son. You need something stabilizing. Someone to come home to." She pulled off a glove and reached for his arm. It was as close to tender as he'd know from her, and it gave him chills. "There's purpose in marriage, and if you're fortunate, love will follow."

Charles swallowed. "Okay. I'll do it."

"Wonderful. I'll call her father tomorrow, and we'll start moving forward."

"Her? Who is her?"

"Cordelia Hendrickson," Irish Colleen answered. She placed the oven mitt back over her hand and reached for her dishes again. "Help me by taking the rolls?"

Charles' head shook. It spun with how quickly everything had changed, with only a few words. "Who is she, though? And why do I know that name? Hendrickson?"

Irish Colleen passed him a bowl of rolls. "That's another story, Charles. For another time, when we don't have guests waiting."

Epilogue: Irish Colleen and the Seven

Collen Deschanel, known as Irish Colleen to her family and friends, peeked her head into the bedrooms of her seven children on Christmas Eve night, one by one, as she did every night of her life.

She visited Charles first, as always. Their conversation from the night before was still fresh, and she ruminated on his words and intentions, which had seemed to come from the right place. Her oldest would never tell her anything. She might never know what sent him to come see her, but God worked in mysterious ways. He was on the right path now, and that was all that mattered.

Soon, she would need to tell him about Cordelia... about her father. That could come later.

Habit made her pause briefly at Augustus' door before she remembered. He was a man now, with his own successful business, and, as Elizabeth had astutely observed, he needed to forge his own way. It was too late for her to wonder where she could have stepped differently with Augustus; how she could have made different choices, nurtured him better. He might never know the anguish of a parent caught questioning their shortcomings. She feared his path would be lonely, and worse, that he would choose this above feeling anything real.

Irish Colleen brushed the handle of his door with her palm and moved on.

Colleen wasn't alone in her room. Evangeline lay sideways across her sister, a mess of curls and tangled limbs. Evangeline wouldn't sleep under this roof for much longer. She'd made her intentions known to move in with Augustus after the New Year and had dared anyone to challenge her decision.

No one had. Augustus needed Evangeline as much as she needed him. Everyone would sleep better knowing they were caring for one another.

Colleen's hand rested lazily against her sister's back. Soft snores emanated from her, and she was dead to the world, lost to a deep sleep that was so foreign to her. Irish Colleen didn't know the extent of the rift between her girls, and didn't want to, but she knew how important their reunion was. God had given them this miracle, just as God had given her children many mechanisms with which to cope with their highly unusual lives.

Lord knew Irish Colleen had never done well by them in this area.

On this night, the two-year anniversary, Irish Colleen passed by Madeline's door without pausing. Her heart skipped, and her breathing slowed, but she kept moving, because if she couldn't move on, how could she expect her children to?

Maureen was awake, sitting on her bed with a book in her lap. Irish Colleen had been taken aback at how it was fiction, above all else, that her troubled daughter had glommed on to in their homeschooling.

"What are you reading, sis?"

Maureen held up the book without answering. *The Awakening*, by Kate Chopin. Irish Colleen hoped it wasn't too racy.

She blew her daughter a kiss, their thing. Maureen grimaced, and Irish Colleen started, heartsick, to back out of the room. And then Maureen blew a kiss back, and all was right.

For tonight, anyway.

As always, Irish Colleen stopped last at Elizabeth. Her baby, Lizzy. The tortured one.

There were no dormer windows here at Ophélie; no moonlight to spill through and illuminate the path to her youngest's room. No symbols to interpret, or to lose precious sleep deciphering.

Irish Colleen stepped inside. Elizabeth sat in her window seat, a crude wooden bench that Charles had crafted for her himself and stapled one of her cushions to. It had all the charm of a popsicle stick house, but Elizabeth treated it as if it were a royal throne.

"Better get to sleep, or Santa won't come," Irish Colleen teased.

Elizabeth turned and leveled a look on her. "I'm too old for Santa, Mama."

"I know that," Irish Colleen said quickly. "Of course you are."

"Sure." Elizabeth was a teenager now, in every way. Gone was the soft innocence of a child who needed her comforts. In its place was sarcasm and eye rolls. Impatience and the weariness of indulging an insufferable parent. Irish Colleen had endured this with all her seven, but Elizabeth was her last, the baby, and the realization she was no longer needed in the same way was an unexpected punch to the gut.

"It's late," Irish Colleen said. She sat next to Elizabeth on the bench, but carefully. She feared the whole thing would fall apart with little provocation. "I'm not fussing, Lizzy, you know that." Proving herself wrong, she brushed her hand through Elizabeth's stringy hair. She was at an age where she should be taking more interest in her appearance and practicing better hygiene. The time would come soon; maybe if Connor kept coming around she'd see he was more than her childhood friend. She'd see the way Irish Colleen noticed him looking at her baby.

Elizabeth recoiled, but forced a smile as she dodged her mother's ministrations. "Stop. Come on." She pulled her hair over her shoulder. "I'll go to bed soon. Just thinking."

"About Maddy?"

She shrugged. "I guess. We shouldn't have let Augustus go home alone tonight."

Irish Colleen tensed. "Is there something I should know?"

"Not premonition, Mama, just saying. He'll never be okay at Christmas again. Never."

She nodded and wrapped her sweater tighter. Outside, rain pummeled the grass and trees, and a wind whipped through, singing a whistling song. "No, I don't suppose any of us will."

"Evie is good for him. He'll be okay..."

Irish Colleen felt and heard the hesitation at the end... the very clear *for now.* She wouldn't press. Couldn't.

"Charles will be married soon," Irish Colleen said. She didn't know why she chose to announce it to her youngest before any of the others. Except she did. It was why she'd always broached adult topics with Elizabeth... leaving the sentence open ended, an invitation to offer her anything that might help steer her toward or away from terrible decisions.

"Yeah," Elizabeth said, for of course she already knew.

"I think Colleen may be looking at colleges abroad."

"Scotland."

"Yes, Scotland," Irish Colleen said. "Once she goes, and Charles is married, it will be only you, me, and Maureen. This home is your brother's, and we'll need to step aside when he has his own family. I was thinking we might move into one of the townhomes your father's family owns. One of those pretty colorful numbers on Esplanade. Or, we could buy a new one."

"Yeah, sure."

"You don't have an opinion?"

"On where we live, or the fact that Charles is marrying the woman who will be the end of him?"

And there it was... what she had come for. The words that would cool her blood and give her fresh worries for the coming year. "What do you know about it?"

"I know what you already know, Mama. Knowing won't change anything. You could call it off tomorrow and fate would find a way to bring them together, because fate is written in the stars."

"You mean God's plan."

Elizabeth's laugh chilled her. "If believing God is behind this makes all this easier, by all means, blame him."

"Lizzy, mind your tongue. He is always listening. He loves you."

Elizabeth turned toward her mother. She was not a girl on the eve of thirteen as the lightning lit her face, but a woman hardened by the burdens no one could carry for her. "Tell me again in a few years if you still believe He loves any of us."

Also by Sarah M. Cradit

KINGDOM OF THE WHITE SEA

Kingdom of the White Sea Trilogy

The Kingless Crown

The Broken Realm

The Hidden Kingdom

The Book of All Things

The Raven and the Rush

The Sylvan and the Sand

The Altruist and the Assassin

The Melody and the Master

The Claw and the Crowned

THE SAGA OF CRIMSON & CLOVER

The House of Crimson and Clover Series

The Storm and the Darkness

Shattered

The Illusions of Eventide

Bound

Midnight Dynasty

Asunder

Empire of Shadows

Myths of Midwinter

The Hinterland Veil

The Secrets Amongst the Cypress

Within the Garden of Twilight

House of Dusk, House of Dawn

Midnight Dynasty Series

A Tempest of Discovery

A Storm of Revelations

A Torrent of Deceit

The Seven Series

1970

1972

1973

1974

1975

1976

1980

Vampires of the Merovingi Series

The Island

and more

The Dusk Trilogy

St. Charles at Dusk: The Story of Oz and Adrienne

Flourish: The Story of Anne Fontaine

Banshee: The Story of Giselle Deschanel

Crimson & Clover Stories

Surrender: The Story of Oz and Ana

Shame: The Story of Jonathan St. Andrews

Fire & Ice: The Story of Remy & Fleur

Dark Blessing: The Landry Triplets

Pandora's Box: The Story of Jasper & Pandora

The Menagerie: Oriana's Den of Iniquities

A Band of Heather: The Story of Colleen and Noah

The Ephemeral: The Story of Autumn & Gabriel

Bayou's Edge: The Landry Triplets

For more information, and exciting bonus material, visit www.sarahmcradit.com

The Family

Deschanel Family (Line of August)

The Deschanel (*pronounced Day-shah-nell*) family are the line of heirs of the great Charles Deschanel of France, who settled the Deschanel dynasty in Louisiana in 1844. All current day descendants of this original Charles are either of the line of August or Blanche. Deschanels are of the line of August, and all others (Fontenots, Broussards, Guidrys, etc.) come from Blanche. August, with his wife "Irish" Colleen Brady, had seven children: Charles, Augustus, Colleen, Madeline, Evangeline, Maureen, and Elizabeth. Madeline, their fourth child, tragically passed in an automobile accident on Christmas morning, 1970.

Irish Colleen was August's second wife. His first, Eliza, he married for love, but she was unable to bear children and eventually passed away from cancer.

The rights of inheritance of the Deschanels follow the tradition of the eldest son, so Charles, son of August, is the current heir.

August (1905-1961) & "Irish" Colleen Brady (1932-)

Charles b. 1950
Augustus b. 1951
Colleen b. 1952
Madeline b. 1953
Evangeline b. 1954
Maureen b. 1956
Elizabeth b. 1959

Deschanel-Broussard Family (Line of Blanche)

The Deschanel-Broussard family (*pronounced Brew-sard*), are cousins of the Deschanel family, equal in wealth and prestige. Where the Deschanels are descendants of the line of August, the Broussards are descendants of the line of Blanche. Claudius Broussard is Blanche's third husband, and the children from this union are considered her most favored. She also has a son by her second husband, Johnson Guidry, but her relationship with Pierce is fractured.

Blanche did not have children by her first husband, Ellis Kenner. Both Ellis Kenner and Johnson Guidry died of "mysterious circumstances."

Blanche Deschanel (b. 1906) & Johnson Guidry (1890-1930)
Pierce b. 1926

& Claudius Broussard (b. 1900)
Eugenia b. 1940
Pierce b. 1926
Cassius b. 1942
Wyatt (1943-1955)
Noble (1944-1955)

Guidry Family (Line of Blanche)

The Guidry family are those descended from Pierce Guidry, first son of Blanche Deschanel-Broussard. Although the first son is the heir on the Deschanel side, Blanche does not recognize Pierce as her heir. Instead, she sees her second child and eldest daughter, Eugenia Fontenot, as her heir. Pierce represents his line of the family as one of the seven Deschanel Magi Collective Council. His two daughters, Pansy and Kitty, are also on the Council.

Of Pierce's children, only Pansy, so far, is married.

The Guidrys, for no reason other than Blanche's disdain for her second husband, Johnson, are considered the black sheep of the clan.

Pierce Guidry (b. 1926) & Winnifred Babin (b. 1926)

Pansy b. 1949 (m. Placide Lafont b. 1945)

Alton b. 1950

Kitty b. 1954

Fontenot Family (Line of Blanche)

The Fontenot family are those descended from Eugenia Broussard-Fontenot, second daughter of Blanche Deschanel-Broussard. Although Eugenia is a second child, and a daughter to boot, Blanche recognizes Eugenia as her heir. Eugenia is married to Wallace Fontenot, and they have three sons. Eugenia represents her line of the family as one of the seven Deschanel Magi Collective Council.

The Fontenots are well-respected in the community, with a similar prestige as their Deschanel cousins.

Eugenia Broussard (b. 1940) & Wallace Fontenot (b. 1939)

Luther b. 1962

Llewellyn b. 1963
Lowell b. 1964

Broussard Family (Line of Blanche)

The Broussard family are those descended from Cassius, third child and second son of Blanche Deschanel-Broussard. Cassius is married to Helene Barrow, and they have two children, a son and a daughter. Cassius represents his line of the family as one of the seven Deschanel Magi Collective Council.

The Broussards, like the Fontenots, are well-respected in the community, with a similar prestige as their Deschanel cousins.

Cassius Broussard (b. 1942) & Helene Barrow (b. 1944)
Jasper b. 1963
Imogen b. 1965

Sullivan Family

The Sullivans are one of the oldest and most trusted families in New Orleans. A family of attorneys, a majority of Sullivans, most notably males until recently, join the family law firm, Sullivan & Associates, which has been a New Orleans staple since 1839. The family came up through the ranks, by their bootstraps, with humble beginnings as Irish immigrant laborers. The Sullivans are both the attorneys and friends of the Deschanel Family. Like the Deschanels, the designation of heir follows the eldest son, and so Colin Sullivan Sr. is considered the head of the family. His father, Patrick, still lives, but in quiet retirement.

Colin Sullivan Sr. (b. 1932) & Josephine Bartleby (b. 1931)

Colin Sullivan Jr. b. 1950
Rory Sullivan b. 1952
Patrick Sullivan b. 1953
Chelsea Sullivan b. 1956

Sullivan & Associates

Sullivan & Associates is a family-owned law firm, and one of the oldest and most trusted in New Orleans, founded in 1839 by Aidan Sullivan. Comprised mostly of Sullivans, the firm is considered something of a birthright for any Sullivans looking to go into law. They have represented the Deschanel interests for over a century. Charles Deschanel's best friend, Colin Sullivan Jr., as well as Colin's two brothers, Rory and Patrick, all plan to join the family firm one day. Colin Sullivan Sr. is the current Senior Partner, following the retirement of his father, Patrick. Colin Sr. and his brothers, Jerome and Jamie, are the figureheads of the firm.

Homes & Properties

Oak Haven

The old Victorian mansion Irish Colleen and seven children reside in, on Chestnut and Sixth in the Garden District, just beyond Lafayette Cemetery No. 1. Although there are larger (Magnolia Grace) and more storied (Ophélie) homes in the family possession, August Deschanel chose this particular property to raise his family in with the thought of giving them a more "normal" upbringing than he had.

The Gardens

The colossal mansion of Ophelia Deschanel at Jackson Ave., taking up an entire square block between Coliseum and Prytania in the Garden District. The Gardens also houses the cavernous chambers where the Deschanel Magi Collective and the Collective Council meet to discuss family business. The architectural style of the estate is Italianate, and the most notable feature is the extensive, exotic garden wrapping around the property, shielding the home from outside view. This house will be inherited by the future Deschanel Magi Collective Magistrate.

Ophélie

A large plantation and surrounding lands purchased by Charles Deschanel I, built in 1844, and currently occupied intermittently by the Deschanel family. Charles will inherit the property as the heir to the estate. Located near Vacherie, an hour west of New Orleans, the Greek Revival ivory mansion on the Mississippi River is secluded from the road by gates and foliage. The estate has forty-five rooms and large ornate gardens, as well as two hundred outbuildings from when the property was a working plantation.

Magnolia Grace

A beautiful, traditional Greek Revival mansion in the Garden District that once belonged to Fitz Deschanel (the second son of Charles I), and has ever since been passed down through the second sons. Augustus Deschanel is set to inherit this property, which is located on Prytania, near Eighth.

Deschanel Media Group

The brainchild of Augustus Deschanel, who had dreamed of starting his own company since he was a young boy. The company's vision is a magazine for locals, which both catered to the elites but also offered an opportunity for aspiring writers to get their short stories published and in front of potential patrons. Augustus currently has no employees but himself, though Evangeline has been busying herself by offering him free help.

Femme Forte

A sprawling Northshore mansion along Lake Pontchartrain, considered the birthright of Blanche and her descendants. The property will be inherited by Eugenia Fontenot, her favorite child.

Weatherly Estate

The vast, columned Uptown home of Daniel Weatherly Sr., gifted for his patronage of Tulane. His son, Dan Jr., is a good friend of

Charles Deschanel. The estate is located near the sister universities of Tulane and Loyola, by the Ursuline's Academy.

Also by Sarah M. Cradit

KINGDOM OF THE WHITE SEA

Kingdom of the White Sea Trilogy

The Kingless Crown

The Broken Realm

The Hidden Kingdom

The Book of All Things

Blackwood Cycle

The Raven and the Rush

The Poison and the Paladin

Southerlands Cycle

The Sylvan and the Sand

The Flame and the Forsaken

Guardians Cycle

The Altruist and the Assassin

The Belle and the Blackbird

Darkwood Cycle

The Melody and the Master

The Hand and the Heart

Sceptre Cycle

The Claw and the Crowned

THE SAGA OF CRIMSON & CLOVER

The House of Crimson and Clover Series

The Storm and the Darkness

Shattered

The Illusions of Eventide

Bound

Midnight Dynasty

Asunder

Empire of Shadows

Myths of Midwinter

The Hinterland Veil

The Secrets Amongst the Cypress

Within the Garden of Twilight

House of Dusk, House of Dawn

Midnight Dynasty Series

A Tempest of Discovery

A Storm of Revelations

A Torrent of Deceit

The Seven Series

Nineteen Seventy

Nineteen Seventy-Two

Nineteen Seventy-Three

Nineteen Seventy-Four

Nineteen Seventy-Five

Nineteen Seventy-Six

Nineteen Eighty

Vampires of the Merovingi Series

The Island

and more

The Dusk Trilogy

St. Charles at Dusk: The Story of Oz and Adrienne

Flourish: The Story of Anne Fontaine

Banshee: The Story of Giselle Deschanel

Crimson & Clover Stories

Available as a single collection, The Shorts

Surrender: The Story of Oz and Ana

Shame: The Story of Jonathan St. Andrews

Fire & Ice: The Story of Remy & Fleur

Dark Blessing: The Landry Triplets

Pandora's Box: The Story of Jasper & Pandora

The Menagerie: Oriana's Den of Iniquities

A Band of Heather: The Story of Colleen and Noah

The Ephemeral: The Story of Autumn & Gabriel

Bayou's Edge: The Landry Triplets

For more information, and exciting bonus material, visit www. sarahmcradit.com

About the Author

Sarah is the USA Today and International Bestselling Author of over forty contemporary and epic fantasy stories, and the creator of the Kingdom of the White Sea and Saga of Crimson & Clover universes.

Born a geek, Sarah spends her time crafting rich and multilayered worlds, obsessing over history, playing her retribution paladin (and sometimes destruction warlock), and settling provocative Tolkien debates, such as why the Great Eagles are not Gandalf's personal taxi service. Passionate about travel, she's been to over twenty countries collecting sparks of inspiration, and is always planning her next adventure.

Sarah and her husband live in a beautiful corner of SE Pennsylvania with their three tiny benevolent pug dictators.

www.sarahmcradit.com

www.ingramcontent.com/pod-product-compliance
Lightning Source LLC
Chambersburg PA
CBHW020334310726
48979CB00015B/2367/J
* 9 7 8 1 9 5 8 7 4 4 2 5 3 *